ANNA
AND THE
LOST
ZORN

HANS M HIRSCHI

Beaten Track
www.beatentrackpublishing.com

Anna and the Lost Zorn
First published 2023 by Beaten Track Publishing
Copyright © 2023 Hans M Hirschi

All rights reserved.

Paperback ISBN: 978 1 78645 578 9
eBook ISBN: 978 1 78645 579 6

Beaten Track Publishing,
Burscough, Lancashire.
www.beatentrackpublishing.com

− FOREWORD −

This is something I have not done before. I'm inclined to blame my zodiac—I'm a Gemini—for always wanting to try new genres and new ideas. In reality, it's probably not that simple. It never is, but after years of nagging by readers, I finally caved in and decided to attempt to write a crime novel.

Writing crime, however, has proven to be challenging for an author with my style of creating. Crime and "stream of consciousness" do not go well together, and the plotting and constant checking that I wasn't giving away too much too soon proved strenuous. I don't think I've ever worked so hard on a book before. While it did take some of the pleasure out of the process, I think I've learned more about the craft that is writing. This is also the first time that my main character isn't male, and that was scary, too. Making sure Anna is as flesh-and-blood as a fictional character can be was important to me for the credibility of the story. At the end of the day, I'm very proud of it. It's crime, but it's crime "my way."

Another important character is the location where the story largely plays out, Styrsö, the island where I have lived since 1996. Alas, writing about your neighborhood is more difficult than I imagined. Despite how long I have lived here, I still don't know the names of every corner, nook, and crevasse, and given that some of my neighbors might actually read this, I dare not make mistakes or I'd face the wrath of my community. Hence the research into this book is much more focused on small details than ever before.

Wanting to stay on this island that has been home for more than a quarter of a century, I also had to be mindful of what I say and how I express it. Which social issues are okay to mention, and which lines must not be crossed? I have spent hours debating self-censorship with friends and loved ones. Because as much as we value freedom of speech and expression—and we do have that freedom—there are consequences for the things we say and do, warranted or not. Not everybody takes kindly to criticism, and there are taboos in every society, not just here. I hope I have struck the right balance. Nobody mentioned in the book exists in real life, with two exceptions, and they have given me their express approval. Any other similarities you might find are purely coincidental and not by design.

I remember my first visit to Styrsö, in the late summer of 1996. The crime I committed then (as the islands were still a restricted military zone and foreigners were only allowed after applying for a permit from Sweden's security police and the armed forces) by coming here to look at a house to buy without securing a permit* has hopefully expired under the statute of limitations.

I dared not speak on the ferry for fear of my accent giving me away and people realizing I'd only lived in Sweden for four years. I also remember feeling this strong sense of coming home when I stepped off the ferry. When my partner at the time and I revisited the island the coming weekend and strolled around, I felt this calm descend upon me, this sense of belonging. It's not always been like this, and there were times when we just wanted to up and leave (and we did, albeit briefly).

However, we did return, and in the years since, Styrsö has become a part of my family. Yes, there are conflicts; we argue at times, and we don't always see eye to eye, but when I sit and contemplate things on a rock or at the beach in Brännholmsviken, looking out over the sea toward the west, that's when I am as much at peace as I could ever hope for.

Styrsö is my home! It's where I want to grow old and where, one day, my ashes will be spread at sea.

The author

*I did apply for and received a permit after we had purchased the house in the fall of that same year. On April 1st of 1997, the military restrictions were lifted, and tourists are welcome to visit the islands today. I applied for and was granted Swedish citizenship in 2001.

– PROLOGUE –

Late in the evening of September 5, 2022

WHAT A DAY it had been. Crazy! The police had come almost immediately and begun an extensive missing-person search. They'd even called in a helicopter with an infrared camera. Not surprisingly, they didn't find anything. Just an hour ago, they'd left the island but would be back again tomorrow with dog teams and divers.

It was troubling. Part of a string of small islands just off the coast, with quaint settlements, old houses, narrow streets, stunning landscapes, and views, Styrsö was such a beautiful and usually very peaceful place. Whoever set foot on the island would quickly fall in love; some would stay forever. That peace had been brutally disturbed by the police presence. Would people ever forget? Forgive?

Salskärs Udde would undoubtedly be where the police divers began their search tomorrow. It was the most logical place. It was so soothing to look out over the sea, beyond the westernmost islets, to the ever-expanding horizon. The sea level was unusually low, due to a high-pressure system that had summer lingering longer this year, and it was still warm outside, temperatures reaching almost seventy-five degrees, despite the early September date.

It was a stark reminder of how rapidly the climate was changing. White winters, the sea frozen solid, people driving their cars to the islands...were but a distant memory. Sure, the archipelago still saw snowfall every winter, but more often than not, it melted the second it hit the ground.

In the far background lay Styrsö's large forest. One hundred and fifty years ago, barely a tree stood there, all chopped down in centuries past to build ships to brave the surrounding ocean. The sea had always provided for the people living there—merchant sailors, fishermen, and their families.

The sea was also a burial place, a cemetery, and had just served in that capacity again. A couple of miles off the Swedish West Coast, Styrsö was the largest of the islands in Gothenburg's southern archipelago and had been inhabited for thousands of years. It had seen many people buried over the ages, on land and at sea.

Today, Mother Nature had provided a helping hand, supplying everything necessary: an ocean where a body could be disposed of with virtually no chance of it ever appearing again, foggy conditions to hide the deed, temperate salty water, and countless sea creatures that would aid the rapid decomposition of the corpse. A deep sigh escaped as thoughts of the victim flashed before the inner eye.

As a student of the island's history as well as having been raised on the island, it had always been fascinating to witness how the entire Scandinavian peninsula had slowly risen from the ocean after the weight of the latest Ice Age was lifted from its shoulders, slowly altering the landscape, unearthing oceanic secrets, giving way to smooth rock faces ground by water and gravel pushed along by the slow flow of the glaciers, and carving out valleys where green meadows now stood.

The island had been growing in size for ten millennia; indeed, the entire West Coast of Sweden rose by about a millimeter every year. Only in recent decades had the global increase in sea levels overtaken the rising effect, almost imperceptibly submerging islands and coastlines again as Mother Nature reclaimed what was rightfully hers, albeit due to human interference. By the time the ocean reached the places it had retreated from only a short time ago—in the comparably long life of the planet—everybody living on the island today would be long gone. The sea would take back the land and hold on tight to every earthly secret, as it had the corpse sunk into its depths just hours ago.

Tiny waves lapped ashore around the figure sitting silently on the rounded rock protruding from the sea. The water was cool, sixty-three degrees at the most, but some people still bathed. It had long been a tradition among locals to winter bathe, but not out here at Salskärs Udde. There were better places for that, with sandy beaches or ladders. Nobody came here this late in the evening to disturb the quiet and peaceful view due west toward the small island of Vinga with its famous lighthouse.

After a final look out toward the spot where the body had been disposed of, it was time to head home and prepare for what was to come. Undoubtedly, the police would ask more questions, and they would turn the island upside down in their search. They would fail. In time, they would turn their backs on Styrsö, and the island would move on, as it had so many times before. People would go back to their regular lives and the hourly pulse of the arrival or departure of the ferries that briefly filled the roads with traffic.

− 1 −

September 5, 2022

WHEN ANNA WALKED into her apartment, it was already dark outside. Her PR executive job kept her busy beyond what most people in Sweden would consider regular hours. She'd been working for Stockholm's most successful advertising and PR firm for several years now, quickly rising through the ranks with an uncanny ability to hit the right tone for her clients' campaigns, be it online or in print. With Sweden's elections coming up in less than a week, she was busy assisting one of their newest clients, one of Sweden's parliamentary parties, to cut through the media frenzy and make a dent, hopefully increasing their share of votes in the election.

One of the smaller parties in Sweden's parliament, and considered fringe by many, they found it hard to be seen or heard. Anna's reputation had preceded her, and the firm had been approached to help them out. Initially put off by the prospect of working with a party she couldn't personally identify with, she'd fallen for the witty charm of the party's secretary general, who had been in charge of hiring a new firm. Anna had put together a concept that had been approved, and here they were: six days away from election day. So far so good. The party's poll numbers were better than they had been a few months ago, but in the end, the only thing that mattered was the number of votes cast in the election. Voter turnout was one of their final campaign's main focuses.

She'd been so busy with the crazy frenzy of the day's work that she'd had no time to check her mail or voice messages. She regularly turned her personal line off during the day so she could work without unwanted interruptions.

Walking into the empty apartment was depressing. She turned on the lights, but that didn't make things any better; quite the contrary. Her apartment didn't feel like home, never had, even though it was in one of the hipper neighborhoods of Stockholm, an expensive condo paid for with her large corporate salary. She'd moved to Stockholm, following her dream of a better job, more responsibility, and a lot less family drama, leaving behind a few friends and her entire family in Gothenburg, on the other side of the country. Despite having lived here for more than a decade, Stockholm wasn't home, and her apartment still felt like a hotel room rather than her own four walls. There were no plants, no personal decorations, no art, and no family photos.

She contemplated her move as the fridge turned out to be as barren as her love life. There was no food and no significant other. Why she bothered to look was beyond her. She knew it was empty before opening the door, and while the former was by accident or perhaps oversight, the latter had been entirely by design. The last fling she'd had was a couple of months ago with a bartender. The sex had been amazing, but that was it. They had nothing in common apart from their insatiable lust for sex. After a couple of weeks, the two women parted amicably, having grown tired of "same, same."

Before that, there had been Anton, the mysteriously quiet guy from Latnivaara who'd moved to Stockholm to study archeology. They'd seen each other off and on for almost a month, but Anton was more interested in digging out fossils than exploring Anna. She'd dumped him in a text. She barely remembered most of the other people who'd come through her door, revolving more than it ever stayed shut, every few weeks a new plaything, but nobody hung around long enough to get to know her. She didn't mind—no. She made sure they didn't. It was who she was.

The weirdest thought cut through from deep within her subconscious: did she even qualify for relationships? Anna shrugged. She didn't care for one to begin with. Relationships were overrated anyway, designed as they were to subject the likes of her to male superiority and persistent heteronormative roles. She didn't need a man to tie her to a stove for the remainder of her life. Nor did she, butch as she felt she was, need some meek little femme as her arm candy at public events. *Shudder!*

She picked up her phone to check out the latest offers from the delivery service. *Maybe I'll get lucky and the cute Somali guy will drop off my food again?* The last time he'd been there, she'd topped off her tip by letting him fuck her against the hallway wall. It gave the word *quickie* a completely new meaning. Anna laughed at the thought. She didn't even bother to get his name, but his dick had proven to be most memorable. Absentmindedly, she licked her lips as she placed her order for Indian takeout.

Turning her personal line back on, her screen almost instantly went crazy with various notifications, and she noticed her father had texted her. Again. Anna let out a long sigh. She was too busy for his drama today. When he called yet again, she went to swipe him away but accidentally pressed the wrong button and answered instead.

"Anna, it's Dad."

"Yeah, I can see that. What is it?" He was the last person she wanted to talk to today, or any day really, let alone see his face on her small screen.

"All my calls went straight to voice mail, and you've not responded to any of my texts."

"I've been busy. I told Pa weeks ago, didn't I? We're days away from the election, and I'm swamped with work. Can't it wait until Monday?"

"Pa is missing!" Anna heard her father's voice crack on the other end of the line, and looking more closely at the screen, she could see he'd been crying. He seemed to have aged a decade since she'd last talked to him. Then again, that had been a few months ago.

"What do you mean, missing?" She didn't have time for his antics today, even less so than she would've any other day of the year.

"He left for his walk this morning and he's not been back since."

Anna sat down, hitting the chair hard as the muscles in her legs suddenly refused their service. She'd always been closer to Pa than she was to Dad. "Did you talk to the police? What do they say?"

"Of course. Who do you think I am?" Her father was now openly crying, wailing almost.

"What did they say?" Her voice came out hard and cold as she tried to hang on to a semblance of control.

"They arrived about an hour ago. They want me to be patient. To look for him, talk to neighbors and friends. It's not like I haven't been doing all of that. I've walked across the entire island again and again ever since I came back from my appointment in town. Half the island has been looking for him. We've been to every one of his favorite spots. Nothing. I don't know what to do! I can't live without him."

His wailing shook Anna to the core. Her father had always been a bit of a drama queen, but she'd never seen him like this before. Nor was Pa the sort of person who'd just leave the house without telling his husband of almost fifty years where he was going. This was completely out of character for him. She could see how Dad would be upset.

Anna felt her heart break at her father's tears, his despair, and she knew she only had one choice: to get home as quickly as she possibly could.

"Dad, listen! I'll get on the first flight out. But to do that, I need to hang up so I can book my flight. I'll call you once I'm on my way. Okay? Just give me a few minutes." She detected the slightest hint of relief on the other end, but no words confirmed the information she'd relayed. "I'll call you back shortly. Hang in there!" She hung up.

Finding a flight at this time of night was easier said than done. It was eight forty-five already, and she quickly realized that the last plane would leave Stockholm in less than an hour.

Just getting to the airport would take that long. She could take the night train to get her to Gothenburg at seven a.m., but she might as well take the first flight in the morning. She could take a car to Gothenburg but realized her biggest obstacle: getting to the island in the middle of the night. The last ferry left Saltholmen after midnight, and there was no chance she'd get there in time. And the first one in the morning didn't leave until six a.m. Unless...

Frantically packing an overnight bag, she called her childhood friend who lived on the island. "Sven?"

"Anna? To what do I owe the pleasure?" His hearty laughter always had the same effect on her. Her heart would skip a beat and she'd feel better. Always. Right now was no exception.

"Pa is gone. I guess you've heard?"

"Yeah, I have. I've been helping Tore look for him all afternoon."

"Do you still have your boat?"

She sensed Sven's confusion across the entire country. "Why do you ask?"

"I'm getting a car, driving down right now. I should be there at around two a.m. Can you pick me up, please?"

"I guess, but what difference does it make? Honestly, you haven't been here in years, and suddenly you expect the world to revolve around you?" He seemed stingy. "I don't mind picking you up, but you won't make any difference in the middle of the night. It's too dark to look for Lennart now anyway, and besides, there isn't a place we haven't checked, double-checked, and triple-checked. We have to wait for the police to start their search again in the morning. They're expected to do a sweep with the police helicopter tonight, and then in the morning, the dogs will do their thing. They'll also use divers. Apart from that, there's not much they can do."

"I want to be there for Dad," Anna tried, but even she had to concede the point Sven was making.

"Look, Anna, if it makes you feel better, of course I'll pick you up. I was just about to go check in on Tore, make sure he's eating and getting some rest. These past few hours have been a nightmare for him, especially since you never returned his calls or messages."

"I know, I know! I feel awful. I've been so busy with the election—"

"Anna, he's your father. I know you haven't been close, but still."

She was upset by his admonishment. "Look, Sven, I called my best friend for a favor, not to play a game of 'blame the awful daughter.' Or do I need to remind you of some of your fuck-ups? Plenty to choose from over the years! Can you please just promise to pick me up?"

A loud sigh was the only response she got.

"Thanks, Sven. I'll call you as soon as I know my arrival time at Saltholmen." She hung up.

Next, a car. She didn't own one. Why would she? Living on Södermalm in Stockholm, she had several bus routes and the subway within comfortable walking distance, and everything else was either delivered or she could take an Uber on the off chance she had to visit a store in the suburbs. It made living in Stockholm very convenient. *So very unlike Styrsö.*

She opened the ride-share app and entered the parameters for her trip. For a while, the service seemed to consider not granting her wish, but then the familiar pattern showed up with the thumbnail of a driver and how long it would take for the car to arrive. Five minutes! *Yikes, I'd better get a move on.* She'd reach Gothenburg at around one forty-five in the morning. She grabbed her bag, phone, and keys, picked up a coat in the hallway, put on her shoes, and left the apartment, hurrying down the two flights of stairs.

Fuck, I need to cancel the food delivery. That, however, turned out to be impossible. She shrugged. Having paid for the food already, she hoped that one of the neighbors would open the door and take it or that the delivery guy would take it home to eat himself. She had no idea if they were even allowed to do that.

Her car pulled up, and the passenger window rolled down. "Are you Anna?"

The driver appeared younger than her, in his mid-thirties, with dark hair, cut really short, and a good-looking, three-day beard. Likely Middle Eastern. A bit stereotypical for a cab driver, but she'd take it.

"Yes, that's me." She smiled and got into the back of the car.

"This is the longest drive I've ever been asked to do," the driver began casually, checking Anna out through the rearview mirror. "How come you're not flying?"

"I missed the last flight out, and I have to get home tonight." *Home?* What an odd word. Was Styrsö still her home, after almost two decades away?

"Family emergency?"

"Yeah, something of the sort." Her answer was as generic as she could muster.

– 2 –

September 5, 2022

I'M ALI, BY the way. Given that we'll be spending the next few hours together, I might as well introduce myself." He had taken them south toward Johanneshov, then turned west to Midsommarkransen where he'd gotten onto the E20 freeway toward Gothenburg. Once in Södertälje, he'd exit onto E4 toward Jönköping, as that route was much quicker. "We'll be there at approximately one-fifty in the morning. I checked the destination. It's a harbor. Do you have family there?"

Anna chuckled at the question. "No, not at the harbor. My parents live on an island off the coast. In the archipelago. A friend's picking me up in his boat. There's no way to take your car to the island. They're practically car-free! We use different forms of transportation island-side." That reminded her to text Sven. She shared her ride with him and added the 1:45 a.m. ETA. She'd have to reconfirm once they were approaching Gothenburg.

"It's funny," Ali said. "There's so much water here in Sweden. I come from Syria. We have mostly desert—at least, where I used to live, in Aleppo, before the war."

Anna's attention was momentarily taken up with mental images of war and destruction and memories of the little Syrian boy, Alan Kurdi, who'd washed up drowned on the shores of Turkey. That picture had been all over the news in 2015, and it seemed so long ago, yet it wasn't even a decade.

"I'm so sorry to hear that. How did you get here?"

"Two friends and I left Turkey on foot, walked undetected into Bulgaria, and made our way north. I came to Sweden in August of 2015."

Anna had the distinct impression he was withholding the details on purpose.

"From the Syrian border, we had to walk."

She was flabbergasted. "To Sweden?"

Ali laughed. "No, but bits and pieces. It was a crazy summer. We were able to catch rides on trucks and took trains when we could afford to, but yeah, we did have to walk all through Denmark. Without the proper tickets, they wouldn't let us on board their trains." He laughed, almost fondly, at the memory.

"Your Swedish is excellent. One might think you'd grown up here."

"In Rinkeby, perhaps."

Anna knew what he was alluding to. His accent was heavy, nicknamed after the infamous suburb north of Stockholm where so many immigrants lived clustered and segregated from other parts of the capital.

"I'm doing okay," he added, "yet here I am, driving an Uber rather than doing my rounds at a hospital."

"You're a doctor?" Anna was surprised.

"I studied medicine in Aleppo, yes. I haven't been able to get my degree validated here yet, what with my transcripts lost during the war. What is it you say in Swedish? Neither fish nor fowl? I can't even work as a nurse since that requires certification as well. So I drive this car and I do other work whenever I can. I have to live and support my mother back in Aleppo. Tonight is a good night." He smiled into the rearview mirror, the white around his dark eyes shining in concert with his white teeth. "But tell me, Anna—that's your name, right? Why do you need to get to Gothenburg in the middle of the night?"

"It's a family emergency. My father has disappeared."

"Disappeared? How come? Is he sick? Suffering from dementia, perhaps?"

Anna could appreciate that what she'd told him didn't make much sense.

"No. At least, I don't think so."

That only made things worse.

"What do you mean? Don't think so? He is your father. You should know if he's well or not."

Anna felt embarrassment creep up her throat and neck, and the tips of her ears were burning hot. "We're not very close. We haven't been for a long time."

Ali shook his head and banged the steering wheel, but he kept his mouth shut, which reminded Anna to call her father. He picked up after one ring. "Dad? It's me. I'm in a car."

"Car?"

"Yeah. I missed the last flight, and the night train wouldn't have been in Gothenburg until seven o'clock in the morning. This was the fastest way home. Sven promised to pick me up at Saltholmen."

"But why the hurry? There's nothing you can do in the middle of the night anyway."

"I know. But I couldn't sit in my apartment and do nothing. I would have gone crazy. I need to be there for you."

"Thanks, dear. I appreciate it. I'll see you later then. Be careful, okay?"

Ali looked back at her again, his confusion showing on his face.

"That was my other father," Anna explained with a. shrug. She was not looking forward to having this particular discussion in the middle of the night.

"Your mother remarried?"

"No."

"Ah, your mom's domestic partner." Ali had indeed learned a lot about Swedish coupling customs.

"No."

"I don't understand…" The look on Ali's face was priceless.

"I know. It's complicated." Anna didn't feel like explaining how she was the daughter of two gay men and a deceased lesbian. Not again. She'd done it a thousand times as a child and growing up. She was tired of always being the odd one.

An uncomfortable silence filled the car as it sped south. There was little traffic on the freeway at this time of day, and darkness had long ago descended upon Sweden. Ali was a good driver, steering his small car with steady hands, yet Anna felt his gaze on her every now and then, and she knew he couldn't let go of the inconsistency in her life's story. It was impossible for him. The pieces of the puzzle wouldn't fit, and it was probably driving him crazy. How could she talk to her father when her father was missing? It seemed to confuse everyone, their thoughts going around in circles as they tried to figure it out.

She'd been in the situation a thousand times with people trying to put two and two together and failing. With Pa being five years older than Dad, people often assumed they were friends, cousins, brothers even. Never did anyone peg them as a married couple. Often enough, she'd been seen as Dad's girlfriend instead. Why was it still so inconceivable that two men could be in love and have children? This was 2022, after all. It was infuriating, to the degree that she suddenly blurted out, "I was talking to my other father. The one who is married to my missing father." Her voice was cold, and every word must've felt like an icy dagger cast at poor Ali, who visibly recoiled from it as if scolded.

For a while, he didn't speak but then said, "We don't have gay people in my culture. It's not proper—" He stopped suddenly, perhaps realizing that these were not words that would endear him to his passenger. "Or that's what the mullahs would have you believe." He shrugged and looked at her again, sheepishly. "My apologies. I didn't mean to cause offense. I don't have any gay friends, not that I know of."

He fell silent, and Anna could tell he was trying to reconcile the information with what he knew. There was still a missing piece to make the picture complete, and she wondered when he'd ask the question everyone else did—was she adopted?—so was surprised when instead he asked, "Were you conceived using surrogacy?"

"No. Apparently, Pa was old-fashioned this one time. He and his best friend, a lesbian from Denmark, are my biological parents. Sadly, my mother died shortly after giving birth to me. I never knew her, but my dads have always spoken very highly of her."

"You have an interesting family."

Anna laughed. "You think?"

"My family is very different. We are expected to be very close in my culture. Family and family honor are cornerstones of Middle Eastern society. My dad, while the owner of a successful bakery, was a drunkard, and my mom had to support the family more or less on her own. Three boys...can you imagine? And two daughters. I'm the youngest, and I left right after my sixteenth birthday to make it on my own."

"And you made it into medical school?"

"Long story, but yes. I had good grades in school, and I had good mentors. But it was hard. I'm still supporting my family back home. My dad and my two older brothers disappeared early during the Arab Spring. My uncle was killed, too. And because of the war, my mom didn't see a penny in government money. They barely get by."

Anna heard the desperation in Ali's voice. How lucky she was to have been born in one of the world's free, peaceful, and prosperous countries.

"By the way," Ali said, "I think we'll have to refuel when we reach Jönköping. I don't think I have enough gas for the entire trip. This wasn't planned."

"No problem! Let me know if you need a break. I could even drive for a while. Or if you need a coffee or food, I'm happy to buy." Suddenly, she felt bad for forcing Ali on this crazy five-hour drive to the West Coast and then all the way back again, just because she wanted to get there a couple of hours early.

"Thanks." That was all he said before silence once again filled the car as they considered each other's life stories.

Dark landscapes of Sweden flew by outside as they headed south on the freeway. It was hard to know exactly where they were, as the outside displayed little change with only lights in houses along the road adding a bit of contrast. Cars with their headlights on coming from the south made it even more difficult to see. A sign announcing the exit to Nyköping gave Anna some idea of where they were and how much longer they'd be on the road.

Ali seemed to notice it, too. "If you need to take a break, let me know."

"Thanks, Ali," she responded absentmindedly, yet grateful for his kindness.

"Or if you need to talk…" he added, looking back at her again through the mirror.

"Thanks. I'm not sure that talking is what I need right now. Then again, I also understand that you may need the conversation to stay awake. Do you enjoy driving in the dark? I've never done it myself. I hate the darkness."

"It's okay. I work during the daytime in warehouses or on construction sites, and I use this as a side gig at night. It's tough to make enough money to support both my family back in Syria and to pay for all the bills here. I don't really have a choice."

"Wow, two jobs? Is this your car?"

Ali laughed. "No, it's not. It belongs to a friend. I couldn't afford a car. He also drives for Uber sometimes, but he's married with children and doesn't have time at night. So when he goes off his shift, I take over."

"That makes sense. Is it worth it, though? Financially, I mean? I've read a lot about how little you guys get paid, but I don't know."

"It's not a surgeon's hourly pay, that's for sure. As I said, I don't have a choice." He laughed, but Anna noticed there was frustration in the way he'd said it. No choice! She wondered what life must be like when choice was merely an aspiration, a dream. Did she have a choice in what she was doing now? Could she have stayed in Stockholm, ignored her dad's plea, his desperation?

Ignored that Pa was missing? No. Maybe everyone was in the same boat. It might seem they had a choice, but in reality, no one did. It was just that the things they had no choice over differed from person to person.

"Do you mind stopping at the next available rest area? I need to use the restroom."

"Sure, no problem. Maybe you'd like to sit up front, too, afterward? Makes it easier to talk, you know?"

Anna nodded, biting her lip, suddenly overcome by the strangest fear. Afraid of being raped, or worse, murdered. It was the weirdest of sensations spreading through her body, almost paralyzing her, and she started to question what she'd gotten herself into. What if Ali wanted more than to simply drive her to Gothenburg? While she wasn't the typical damsel in distress and was fully capable of defending herself, would she be able to resist him physically? He looked strong enough. Did that even make sense?

She'd had plenty of conversations with her girlfriends about it. Too many of them had been subjected to sexual banter or overtures; others had experienced much more hands-on behavior by various men they knew. None of them agreed on the best way to handle it. Advice would range from "knee to the crotch," "yell at him as loud as you can," to, "just let them get it over with. Don't fight it!" or "simply ignore them, that's the best way to get them to stop." Anna, never consciously having been subjected to unwanted physical advances from men, or women for that matter, found her brain in overdrive, unable to think clearly.

She was relieved when Ali pulled into a gas station minutes later. There were several trucks, and there was a café, still open. She would be safe for now. After a short comfort break, and buying themselves some coffee for the road, Anna decided to play along and took a seat up front, in the passenger seat. It would have been rude to stay sitting in the back when they were going to continue for another four hours. Ali smiled and steered the car back onto the freeway south. They were making good progress, and with Anna now next to him, he kept his eyes on the road while making conversation with her, mostly small talk about life, work, the upcoming elections, and so on.

"Can I ask you something personal?" he finally mumbled.

Here we go. Anna tensed, sensing where this would go. "Sure, go ahead."

"How do you know if someone is gay?" Ali seemed to almost spit out the sentence.

"What do you mean? Are you trying to suss out if you're gay? Or a friend of yours?"

"A friend, a friend. No, not me. I know I'm straight," Ali responded too quickly and with an uncomfortable laugh, but Anna could appreciate why. Given his cultural background, even the accusation of being gay could be dangerous. Protecting himself, even in a country as open-minded as Sweden, made sense, if that were indeed where this was going.

"Well," she began, "the best way is to just ask your friend if you can. Be supportive. Make sure they feel that you aren't judging and that you wouldn't betray their trust. And if you feel they can't be open yet, for whatever reason, maybe you can drop little hints to show that you're an ally, that you don't judge or condemn. For most people in the LGBTQI community, coming out is incredibly difficult, still, even here in Sweden. It most likely always will be. Queer people are never the norm, by the very definition of the word, and when we come out, it completely changes the way people look at us and how they perceive us. Parents have lifelong dreams for their children crushed, and children are afraid that parents might no longer love them or that friends might abandon them. So it's a very big step. Always will be."

"But you're not...?" Ali cautiously continued, making Anna laugh.

"It's not me you're asking about, is it? I'm not the friend?"

"No, no. Not you. I'm sorry. I'm probably overstepping. I was just curious. Since you seem to know so much."

Anna laughed and shook her head. "Well, I do have gay parents, remember? Growing up, I had to come out myself, in so many situations, as the child of queer parents. At first, when I was little, it was just natural, you know? I told people about my fathers and never gave it a second thought. Because to me, having two dads was the norm. I didn't think it was odd or unusual. Then, in kindergarten, I must've noticed how people reacted to me, the discomfort and the silence, and I retreated and rarely spoke about my family.

"Later, as I grew older, I guess I was maybe twelve or thirteen, I started to see the nuances in people's reactions to my parents. How some would inadvertently cringe or the corners of their mouths would twitch, how I wasn't invited to the homes of certain friends or to some birthday parties. It was all very subtle, but still, I began to see patterns.

"At first, I resented my parents for it, for having me. We had a few rough years as a family, lots of arguments and I was a rowdy and rebellious teenager. Then I met Sara, and she made me rethink it all."

Ali looked at her for the first time in minutes, momentarily sizing her up. "So...you're gay, too?"

Anna shrugged. "I hate labels, you know? Call me pan, bi, queer, or whatever. You could also add *aromantic*. I have sexual relationships with people, but I don't fall in love with them, or... I don't know. I mean, I haven't so far, and I can't see that happening to me, but what do I know? I'm perfectly happy as a single right now. I usually just use the word queer if people insist on a label. You know? I'm odd, I'm queer." She shrugged for good measure, taking another swig from her coffee.

The conversation made her think. Yes, she hated labels, yet still, she applied them liberally to herself and others: femme, butch, gay, queer, aromantic. What did they all mean, and why were they so significant yet still so constricting? Anna thought back to her teenage years, her rebellion against her fathers, Dad primarily, suddenly breaking out of the girlie phase with pink accessories, dresses, unicorns, and stuffed animals, instead embracing jeans, T-shirts, and a short haircut, colored purple for good measure. Just to spite Dad, she became a total tomboy, yet she was still aware enough of what body parts, looks, or gestures would get the appropriate responses from boys and girls alike.

Later, after she'd begun her professional career, she learned quickly that presenting in a more feminine way helped her advance, got her better projects and more interesting clients. It also bestowed upon her other professional advantages by colleagues, both men and women, even though men were usually in the position of power. Professional Anna grew her chestnut-brown hair longer, styling it in large, loose curls that fell softly over her shoulders, wore burgundy lipstick to accentuate her subdued but immaculate makeup, and clothes to ever so subtly allude to her feminine bits. She'd been lucky to have been endowed with physical attributes considered highly attractive in all the right places, driving men and women crazy if she wanted to, not by necessarily overtly showcasing the goods, but by simply reminding them they were there, readily available for the right person.

Anna learned to use her femininity to her advantage, and no one stood a chance when she put her combined intelligence and body to work. At the same time, she never fell in love, and sometimes she wondered if she was even capable of love. *Or am I afraid of it?* Did she deny herself the happiness of a loving relationship just to spite her father? Or was she truly incapable of romantic love? *I guess I'll never really know at the rate my life is going.*

While Anna was contemplating her life choices, Ali drove on in silence, perhaps taking the time to process the information he had absorbed. When he finally spoke again, Anna almost spat out her coffee.

"In my culture, you're only considered gay when you bottom, when you're the woman in the relationship. If you top, you're the man, so that is okay."

"You're telling me that only bottoms are considered gay? Tops are considered straight? That's...odd! What about versatile men? What about women?"

It was Ali's turn to shrug. Anna wasn't surprised, though. It was the age-old adage of male sexuality and its supremacy. The active male was supposedly superior to the passive male or female since he was making use of the penis, the mighty phallus. *Men!* She was so tired of the current world order. Even more frustrating was the fact that there was so little she could do to change things.

"Your friend," Anna continued, "what makes you think he's gay? Is it the usual prejudice? Feminine mannerisms, great sense of fashion, love for Eurovision—or did you fuck him or something?"

Ali shook his head vehemently. "No, no, nothing of the sort. I'm just curious. I don't know any gay people. I just don't want to, you know, be sending mixed signals, to be too friendly. I'm still a stranger in this country, and I want to be kind to everybody. But I also don't want them to get the wrong impression."

"Don't worry," Anna made a dismissive gesture. "I don't think you have to worry about that. You look perfectly straight to me. I doubt any gay man would ever hit on you unless you're on Grindr."

"You can tell?"

"Yeah, I guess. I mean you've already told me, and I don't think gay men normally hit on straight men. Plus they have a sixth sense of who's family and who isn't."

"Family?"

"It's a term we use to depict everybody who's LGBTQI. We're all siblings in our fight for equality, not to mention that we constantly fight amongst ourselves, just like siblings do." That last bit was true; she knew that all too well.

"Do your parents know about you?" Ali wondered.

"Yeah, and it's one of the reasons we fight so much. It's a long story."

"We've got time…" Ali looked at her again and smiled. "Unless, of course, you don't want to talk about it."

"No, it's fine. It's my dad. He never came to terms with my sexuality. I mean, it's not that he disapproves of me being pan or whatever. It's more that he expected me to settle down, get married, and have kids. I think he wants grandchildren, and I don't want kids. I think I hate kids. They're so messy, so loud, and so needy. I'd make a lousy mother. But Dad wanted to be a grandfather."

"Your other father?"

"Pa? He found it difficult, too, at first. But then again, he's different. He's always been supportive of who I am as a person, leaving me to do things my way, much more than Dad. Dad was more the sculptor. You know, trying to mold me into the child he'd always wanted me to be? Pa just walked by my side, insanely curious about the person I was growing into. If that makes sense? They are two very different people, a very odd match but a good one."

"And which one is missing right now?"

"My pa." Tears welled up from nowhere, and Anna began to sob.

"Oh, I'm sorry. I didn't mean to make you sad."

Through snivels, Anna managed to say, "It's okay. Not your fault. I just hope we'll find him alive."

– 3 –

September 6, 2022

"A nna, wake up, we're approaching Gothenburg," Ali said gently.

"What?"

"We're almost there. You fell asleep shortly after Linköping, and I let you sleep. But we've just passed the exit to Landvetter Airport, and we'll be in Gothenburg in maybe ten or fifteen minutes."

Anna yawned and stretched as best she could within the confines of the car and her seat belt. "That was quick. What time is it?" she mumbled more to herself than Ali, picking up her phone and noticing the texts on the lock screen. "Shit, it went on *Do Not Disturb* after eleven p.m. I missed Sven's texts." She called him. Sven picked up almost instantly. "Hey, it's me."

"I texted you. I'm about to leave the house. Are you close?"

"Sorry. I fell asleep. Had my phone on silent. Yes, we've just passed Landvetter. Another twenty-five minutes perhaps?"

"Shoot. I better get a move on then. Okay, you drive safely. I'll see you in about half an hour, forty minutes?"

"Great. Thanks for doing this for me."

"Yeah, yeah…" Sven hung up.

"Your friend is coming?" Ali asked.

"Yes, he was still at home. I can't blame him. I wouldn't leave my house in the middle of the night only to have to wait for someone in a cold boat."

As they drove into Gothenburg, passing the large downtown amusement park, the city lay eerily quiet. The lights were mostly turned off, but given the size of the city, there was still enough light from streetlamps and office buildings to signal a silent welcome of sorts.

Ali's eyes grew wide as he noticed the large wooden roller coaster and saw the skyscrapers and all the construction cranes everywhere. "I've never been to Gothenburg before. Is it a nice city?"

Anna shrugged. "It's okay, I guess. As far as cities go, it does have its charm. But there's not much of the old part of town left, you know, not like Stockholm's Gamla Stan. Here it's just little bits here and there. But the people are friendly. I guess that counts for something. Plus they have streetcars."

Ali steered the car through a seemingly abandoned city onto an empty freeway.

"Take a right, here," Anna instructed him as they approached the Tingstad tunnel.

Ali had to abruptly slow down and take a very tight right turn before getting on another highway that led them through a different tunnel away from the downtown area. There was no other car in sight as Ali sped through the tunnel.

He laughed. "This is fun!"

"Just don't get caught..." Anna smiled at him. Ali was going considerably faster than the allowed speed limit.

They drove on, the Göta river to their right, until Anna instructed Ali to take another right turn, taking them down Torgny Segerstedtsgatan and onto Saltholmsgatan. Within minutes, they arrived.

It felt weird for Anna to be back here. She hadn't seen her parents in over a year, and as always, it had ended in a fight. That had been in Stockholm, during their annual visit. She hadn't been down here in over a decade. This time of year, boats were still in the water, and the parking lots filled to the last spot on both sides of the street. No streetcar waiting at the terminus loop, no traffic, not at this time of day, and because of the risk of vandalizing, the ferry company locked the waiting room at night.

"We're here!" Ali beamed. "Now all I have to do is drive back…"

Watching Ali, displaced in a strange city and not knowing what to do, Anna took pity on him. "Are you going to be okay? If you're too tired, you can come with me. We have plenty of space at the house. I feel bad for making you drive back in the middle of the night. Or do you have to work tomorrow?"

"No, actually, I'm off, but I can't impose on you like that. Not under these circumstances."

"Don't worry about that. Seriously, I couldn't live with myself if you fell asleep at the wheel and something happened." Anna had made up her mind, although she already felt her father's disapproval making her ears burn. She also knew that they would fight regardless, so they might as well fight about this. Stay away from the real thing. Plus, maybe with Ali at her side, her father might not go all out in his "you're the biggest disappointment of my life" shtick that he brought into every argument they had.

She pointed to an empty parking spot behind them. "You can park right there. I know the owners of that spot. If they're not here at this time of day, Lasse is probably away on a business trip and they won't need the parking lot. I'll let them know you've parked there."

"I haven't even said I'm staying," Ali replied.

"That's not up for discussion. Seriously. Turn off your app, park the car, and let's go see if Sven's arrived."

"But private parking?" Ali wasn't convinced.

"Don't worry about it. Everybody does it, at least, with people they know. There aren't nearly enough parking spaces here for everybody living on the islands, and there's no visitors' parking anymore. So that's your only option unless you want to walk a mile in the middle of the night. That's where the nearest visitors' parking is." She shrugged and smiled at him. She'd lived here long enough to know all about the parking chaos at Saltholmen. It had driven more residents off the islands than anything else.

Ali resigned himself to his fate, and Anna got the impression that he didn't mind. He must've been exhausted after working a full day and then driving 300 miles through half the night. She simply couldn't have him drive another 300 miles back. She waited while he reversed the car a few feet and then pulled into the empty space with a small wooden signpost warning people that this was indeed a private parking spot. Anna shrugged. She knew Lasse. He wouldn't mind, assuming this was still his spot. She wasn't sure after all these years.

Ali grabbed her bag from the trunk, locked the car, and joined her. "Where to?"

"Let's go this way." She directed her steps toward the entrance to the harbor. In the background, she noticed a couple of anchored ships in the main Gothenburg harbor, and the lights from the infrastructure, cranes, and floodlights, but it was quiet. No sound, which meant that Sven hadn't arrived yet.

They walked out onto one of the main piers and waited. After ten minutes or so, they heard the engines of a boat approach, and when Anna turned around to look toward the noise, she saw the green starboard position light of the approaching boat. She recognized it as Sven's. "Here he comes."

The boat slowed down and turned into the harbor at Saltholmen. Anna waved so Sven knew where they were. Not that there was anyone else waiting at the harbor in the middle of the night.

Sven brought the boat to a complete halt right next to them and threw Anna a rope. "Welcome home, girl. Here, tie us down."

Anna took the rope and expertly tied it to the nearest cleat. "Thanks for picking us up."

"Us? You brought company?" Sven's face reflected the confusion in his question.

"Yes, I did. Sven, meet Ali, my Uber driver. Ali, meet Sven, my childhood bestie." Anna smiled and climbed down into the boat.

"You're bringing your Uber driver to the island? Tore will throw a hissy fit!" Nevertheless, Sven stretched out his hand to Ali, who took it and carefully climbed down into the boat. He almost lost his footing as the boat rocked from the movement. "Careful. I guess you haven't earned your sea legs yet?" Sven joked. "Anna, can you untie the boat? I want to get back to my warm bed."

"Got anyone keeping it warm for you?" She chuckled, knowing full well that Sven had always been as single as she was. Only, in his case, it was because he'd always had a crush on her, loved her, had waited for her, as hopeless as she knew it was. He probably knew it, too, but Sven was Sven. Always had been a stubborn mule.

"That's for me to know and for you to figure out," he replied cryptically.

Anna looked at him again. *Did he just make a joke or is he serious? Has he actually met someone? Now that would be great news!* She loosened the rope from the cleat and threw it into the boat. Expertly, Sven moved the boat away from the wooden pier, turned her around, and sped out toward the open sea.

Ali sat on the bench at the rear of the boat, looking terrified as it flew across the smooth surface of the water while Anna stood next to Sven, holding on to the back of his chair. With the wind in her long dark hair, she relished the smell of the salt in the air, the roar of the engine, and the view of the dark islands, sprinkled with the odd light in some of the homes, slowly growing nearer.

Nobody said anything. Sven was busy navigating, making sure to avoid any shoals or small boulders protruding from the ocean's surface. There were plenty of risks driving a boat at night, even for someone who'd grown up in the archipelago like Sven, someone who knew the waters well. At twenty knots, it didn't take more than a couple of seconds for a mistake to be fatal. Anna knew this and let him focus on his task. Now and then, she turned to make sure Ali was fine. Had she made a mistake asking this stranger to tag along? Had she done it to have someone to protect her from facing her father, or had she done it for altruistic motives, to allow Ali to get some rest? She wasn't sure and didn't trust herself enough to rule out the possibility that her motives were self-serving. Ali seemed to be lost in thought, too. Or maybe he was just scared?

After a good fifteen-minute ride, the boat slowed down and the familiar silhouette of Styrsö appeared before them.

"Do you want me to drop you off at Bratten or Tången?" Sven asked.

"Tången is fine. It's where you live, and I'd have to walk either way. Let's get you back to your warm bed, shall we?" She smiled and put her hand on his shoulder, rubbing it for a while. "I've missed you!" she added, not knowing why. *Am I jealous? About whom? Have I really missed him? It's been ten years!*

Sven continued to steer the boat past the island, which lay mostly in the dark off the port bow, as most homes along the infamous Snobbrännan were summer homes, stately but abandoned off-season. Nobody was here or they were all asleep. Off starboard, Anna noticed Mosskullen, Bästholmen, and then Stora Källö before Sven slowed down for the final approach to the marina at Styrsö Tången.

Here a few lights were on, and Anna marveled at the sight of the old fishing settlement. It was so peaceful and beautiful. Memories of her childhood washed over her, summers at the beach, swimming, playing, and fishing crabs with friends. She'd had such a privileged upbringing out here. Her parents' house was almost halfway between two of the four villages—if you could call them that—on Styrsö. Tången was where the fishermen and their families had always lived. Then there was the actual village, *byn*, which had been a farming community. Bratten, which was the most modern settlement, had been a hotspot for summer guests since the early nineteenth century with its hot- and cold-water baths, lavish restaurants, and hotel, while Halsvik was where most of the summer homes had once been, ranging from small, one-room cabins to large villas where people from the city would spend the summer. Halsvik had a proud history of its own, and it was there, jumping from the main jetty protruding into the bay, where Anna had learned to swim. It was on that jetty that the youth of the island met up during the long summer evenings to swim and talk, and where many of the older generations went for their morning and evening swims all year round. Her family home lay just off Styrsö Tångenväg, the street connecting Bratten and Tången.

After she had helped Sven to tie up the boat at his spot in the marina and they'd locked the cabin, she climbed onto the jetty and helped Ali up. She could tell he was exhausted and totally out of place. She was tired, too, although the adrenaline of the ride and the mixed emotions of coming back here, *home*, almost like the prodigal daughter, were masking it for now. She stretched out her hand to Sven, who yawned as he accepted it, and she yanked him up onto the wooden jetty.

"We'd better get going. It's a good ten- to fifteen-minute walk home." Anna looked at Ali to see if he was moving.

"Yeah, sure, I'm coming. Lead the way."

"Good night, Sven." Anna put her free arm around his neck and hugged him. "Thanks for the ride. I owe you one."

"Big time!" Sven chuckled. "I'll call you in the morning after you've slept in. Good night, Ali. It was nice meeting you."

"Good night, Sven. Thanks for the ride. It was…interesting," Ali said flatly, still in shock from something.

– 4 –

September 6, 2022

"THAT WAS YOUR first boat ride, right?" Anna asked in a hushed voice as she led the way through a small alley between the wooden homes of Tången.

"Could you tell?" Ali gave her a puzzled look. Under the pale-yellow light of the streetlamp, he looked more like a zombie than a human.

Anna laughed at his question. "Yeah, kinda."

"Truth be told, I can't even swim. If I'd fallen overboard, I'd have drowned right there and then."

"Well, you're safely back on dry land, so don't worry." They had reached the hill on top of which Anna's parents lived. "We're almost there, just a couple more minutes."

The front door was unlocked, as was custom still for many island residents, but given that her father knew she was coming, it made even more sense. He was probably fast asleep.

"We need to be quiet. Dad's probably sleeping, and I don't want to startle him."

Anna walked into the house, which lay in darkness except for a small window lamp shining in the kitchen. She took off her shoes and tiptoed into the living room to see if her father was waiting for her. And there he was, sitting in his favorite rocking chair, a blanket over his legs, fast asleep.

"Dad, wake up, I'm home!" She gently patted her father's cheeks and put her other hand on one of his. After a few seconds, he stirred and opened his eyes, looking straight at her.

"Anna, you're home. Thank God!" Then he noticed the dark figure standing behind her. "Who are you?"

Anna intervened before Ali could say a word. "This is Ali. He was kind enough to drive me all the way down here in the middle of the night. I offered him a bed for the night so he didn't have to drive back up after five hours."

Her father got up slowly and smiled. "Of course. That's very kind of you, dear. Welcome to our humble home. My name is Tore. I'm Anna's father." He stretched out his hand for a handshake. Ali took it with both of his, and they shook hands like that. "Let me go make an extra bed for you in the guest room. Anna, your room is all ready if you want to go to bed."

"Let me help you, Dad. You don't have to do this. Maybe Ali could use a cup of coffee or tea instead, while I make the bed?"

"Thanks, Anna. Yes, can I get you anything, young man? Are you hungry?"

Anna disappeared into the hallway. That had gone more smoothly than she'd anticipated. He hadn't even looked at her oddly. Perhaps he was in shock. Whatever the reason, it made things a little easier on her. She didn't want to fight with him, not now; not ever, really. She loved him, but they had become so comfortable always fighting about something, it had become their go-to place. Somehow the two always had that effect on each other, and Pa would sit idly by and watch the spectacle, only ever putting an end to it when it was about to get out of hand and things would have been said that the two would later regret. It had often gone too far when Pa wasn't around. Anna remembered all the horrible things she'd said to her father and, conversely, the words that were spoken at her that had cut through her skin like razor blades, leaving scars for a lifetime. Would she ever be able to forgive Dad for all the pain he had caused her? Would this crisis be an opportunity for them to move on, as a family? She didn't know, and after she was done making Ali's bed in the old guest room, it was with trepidation in her steps that she walked downstairs to join Dad and Ali in the kitchen.

– 5 –

September 6, 2022

ALI LOOKED AT the older man standing in front of him. He was likely in his sixties, although it was quite difficult to pin down the exact age of Europeans. At least, it was to him. Given Tore's daughter's age, which he also found hard to guess but figured to be late thirties or early forties, it made sense to him that her father would be in his sixties. He had also learned in his years living in Sweden that it was rude to ask.

He watched as Tore poured cold water into the kettle and put it on the electric pad to heat it. Ali had happily accepted a cup of tea, hoping it would make sleep come easier, but he wasn't hungry. The entire situation was so surreal to him. Had anyone told him at the start of his shift that he'd end up in a stranger's kitchen on the other side of the country in the middle of the night, he'd have probably laughed at them.

Yet here he was, in an old house, with complete strangers, stuck on an island. Not just that, the man he was looking at was in a state of despair, missing the love of his life, another man, something Ali found almost impossible to reconcile with everything he knew to be true. Tore looked regular enough, very unlike the mental images Ali had of gay men. He knew that Anna and the man standing in front of him had a fraught relationship. She'd told him as much during their journey. All things considered, they should be running around like headless chickens, searching for their missing loved one, not making beds and tea in the middle of the night, going through this ritual of hospitality, a semblance of normalcy, and showing him such kindness.

At the same time, Ali understood the need for this ritual, for the routine. Because what was one to do in the face of such adversity other than cling to the one thing that made life bearable? To hold on to one's humanity? His mother had acted no differently. She still didn't.

He sat at the kitchen table, watching Tore fetch a tea mug for him and then pick out the different varieties of tea bags they had in their pantry.

"I have some chamomile tea here. I understand it helps you relax. Or I have red rooibos tea or plain black tea. What would you like?"

"I'll take the chamomile, please. And thank you for allowing me to spend the night at your house."

"Don't mention it. I'm just grateful to have my little girl here. If…" Tore didn't finish the sentence and began to cry, just standing there between the stove and the kitchen table.

Ali was unsure what to do. Should he get up and hug the old man? Would that be okay, or would it be crossing one of the many invisible lines that framed Swedish customs? He'd experienced a lot of strange cultural differences after arriving in Sweden and a fair amount of racism, and he was unsure if offering a hug would be considered offensive or if he'd be judged if he didn't. Unsure, yet compelled by the man standing in front of him, so clearly in distress, he got up and crossed the distance and simply took Tore in his arms. The man offered no resistance and collapsed in Ali's embrace, sobbing. Ali was deeply touched by the man's suffering and emotional distress.

"It's okay. I'm sure we'll find him alive and well," Ali tried to console.

Anna came into the kitchen, having heard the crying. "Dad, are you okay?" Looking at Ali, she added, "What happened?"

"He was about to say something about your father. He never got to tell me what."

Together, they helped Tore sit down at the table. Behind them, the tea kettle was done and had turned off.

"Dad," Anna kneeled in front of him. "Would you like a cup of tea, too?"

Tore nodded, drying his tears with the back of his hand. "Yes, please, dear."

Anna got up and fetched the kettle and a couple of extra mugs. She poured hot water into them and placed the tea bags inside for her and Tore. Ali helped himself.

For a short while, there was silence in the room as they each watched the tea bags slowly color the hot water a pale yellow, barely visible in the dim light from the kitchen's seventies-style orange lampshade with its white fringe and tassels. The atmosphere was laden with the tension of decades of unspoken truths, pointless arguments, and the fear of mentioning the potential horrors that might await them in the coming hours and days. Would they find Anna's pa? Was he even still alive?

***

Anna was contemplating her father's fate. He'd never been prone to doing anything as drastic as attempting suicide, so she ruled that out, and she'd no reason to believe he'd just get up and leave without saying a word. Had he and Dad been in a fight? Well, they had always had their dustups but never once of the sort that might prompt one of them to leave, or not that she was aware of.

"Dad, can I ask you something? Did you and Pa fight?"

Tore looked at her incredulously. "No! Why would you think that?"

"I don't know. I'm just trying to make sense of why he would disappear. All his things are still here, right?"

Tore merely nodded but added, "None of this makes any sense. There is no reason for him to disappear like this. You know that our marriage was happy. Sure, we had our disagreements and fights. But what normal couple doesn't? And wouldn't you tell your partner that you were leaving them? And why now? After forty-nine years? No, there are only two explanations for him leaving like this. He's either been a victim of a crime or, much more likely, he's had an accident and is lying somewhere out there on the island, waiting for us to find him."

"What have the police said? I mean, it's been hours! Wouldn't they go search for him with a helicopter? Heat cameras?"

"They did, just after nightfall, with a helicopter. They searched for more than two hours, but there was nothing, and the patrols couldn't find anything either. They left shortly after ten p.m., saying they'll be back in the morning with divers and dog patrols. There was nothing more they could do in the darkness. Not after we had already searched on foot all afternoon."

Tore began to cry again. "He probably left the house after breakfast for his regular walk and just didn't come back. I didn't even realize something was off until he didn't show up for supper. Since it's a Monday, I have my appointment with the doctor in town, as you know, and we don't normally eat lunch anymore. I came home at four p.m., and he wasn't here. I texted him and didn't hear anything back. So I called some of his pals, and they hadn't seen him either. That's when I first texted you, to check if you'd heard from him. Then I went out to look for him. I walked the path he usually takes, from here down to Halsvik and then into the forest. Then I checked Styrsö BK's clubhouse, Brännholmsviken, Salskärs Udde…

"He wasn't anywhere, and I was worried, but not worried enough to call the police right away. I had all these explanations— that he'd met a friend and lost track of time. You know how he can be a bit distracted. Or that his phone's batteries were dead, but then I saw his phone was charged, right there on his nightstand. His wallet, everything is still here. That's when I called the police. And then I was in touch with the Pathfinders to do a more thorough search of the island."

"Pathfinders?" Ali questioned.

"They're a group of, let's say, more mature people, most of whom are retired, here on the island who've created this network of beautiful walking and hiking trails in the forest of Styrsö. They all volunteer their time and labor. We have miles and miles of nature hikes now. They're pretty amazing." Tore was palpably proud of the work they'd done. "Lennart is one of them. He's been working with them for almost a decade. So I figured they'd help me look, and they did. For hours. But nothing. Not a trace."

"What about his phone?" Anna knew about her pa being distracted at times. Oftentimes he'd leave his phone at home rather than take it with him. Or he'd forget to charge it.

"Like I said. It's upstairs, turned on and charged, next to his wallet. There are no texts except mine."

"Did you talk to the people at Styrsöbolaget?" Turning to Ali, Anna explained, "That's our ferry company. Maybe he went to town. Once there, all bets are off. He could be anywhere."

"I've spoken to a couple of the mates on board, but they haven't seen him either, and they don't have access to security footage from Saltholmen. Only the police can get access, so that's for them to decide. I'm sure they'll review that tomorrow, but something tells me he's still on the island. Maybe he went to the shore and..." He didn't finish the sentence. They all understood what he meant. Slipping, a stroke, or a heart attack. Depending on where he'd been, he might never reappear. The sea was vast, and there were plenty of strong currents around the island to carry a body far away. Some were washed up on foreign shores, others were never found again. It all depended on the body, the clothing, and other natural circumstances.

"I'm just glad you're here." Tore smiled weakly and put his hand on Anna's. Turning to Ali, he added, "Thank you for bringing my daughter home safely." Turning back to Anna, he looked at her face, cupping it gently. "You look pale. Are you eating?"

Anna extricated herself from Tore's hand. She didn't like where this was going. "Of course I'm eating. I'm just super busy. The elections are this weekend, and I'm buried in work. This—" she gestured around the room "—doesn't help."

It had taken all of fifteen minutes for her dad to criticize her. Fifteen minutes. There was a part of her that wanted to walk out, but then she noticed her father shrinking away from her words and realized she'd raised her voice.

"I'm sorry, Dad. It's not your fault Pa is gone. I didn't mean it like that. But I've been up for almost twenty hours. I'm exhausted."

Tore didn't respond. She'd been too harsh, jumping to conclusions too quickly. She knew that. He meant well, but after all the years of fighting, she automatically went to her default place with him, assuming the worst, casting him as the villain in this parent-child drama of theirs where he was only out to get her. She had completely forgotten that he was her father, loving her, caring for her. *How did we ever end up in this position?*

The conversation had died a quick death, and silence descended once more around the kitchen table, each of the three absorbed in thoughts of their own. After finishing their tea, they went to bed. Anna gave her father a sleeping pill to make sure he got some rest. He would need his wits about him in the coming days. Once she'd shown Ali where the guest room was and provided him with an extra toothbrush and some towels, she turned in herself. She knew she'd get no real sleep tonight but didn't take a pill herself, knowing she'd need to be awake early to get right on top of the search for Pa.

– 6 –

September 7, 2022

ANNA DIDN'T GET much sleep nor did she feel rested, tossing and turning all night in her childhood bedroom. It still had all the girly touches with pink curtains and her dolls. What had she been thinking? Her parents had been more than gracious in allowing her to decorate her room the way she wanted it, and she did have a very girly phase. Later, she didn't care enough about her surroundings to redecorate. Thinking about her apartment in Stockholm, she realized that nothing had changed—she certainly hadn't. She had never even put up curtains and relied on the blinds to provide her with a bit of privacy from potentially nosy neighbors.

She got up and checked the watch on her phone. It wasn't even seven o'clock in the morning, but she noticed that several emails had already arrived. She checked them and deleted all but one, from her boss. The party chair had screwed up in a late-night panel on TV, and they needed to come up with a plan to save their skins. She replied that she wouldn't be working for the next few days due to an urgent family matter. It didn't take many seconds after sending the response before her phone vibrated. Her boss was calling her.

"Good morning, Anders. You're up early!" Anna tried to sound upbeat, as exhausted as she was.

"I need you in the office, stat!" Anders's voice sounded raspy and desperate.

"I can't. I'm at my father's house in Gothenburg."

"You're what?" came the shrieked reply through the phone's speaker.

"My father disappeared yesterday. I have to find him."

"But, but…" was all Anders could muster to that unexpected response from one of his most dependable employees. Or so he'd told her at her most recent appraisal.

"I'm sorry, but this is more important than the election. I'm sure you'll manage just fine without me."

"No, but I can't… You have this special touch. You're the best person for the job. You know how they eat out of your hands…" Anders tried.

"Did you hear what I said? My father is missing. I'm sorry, Anders, but I don't give a shit about work right now!" She hung up before he said anything else and turned off her phone. She didn't need people from work contacting her today. Not her boss, her clients, or anyone else for that matter. She'd use the landline downstairs to make any necessary calls.

Luckily, her dad was still fast asleep as she walked past his bedroom, and the snoring coming in from the guest room indicated that so was Ali. *What am I going to do with him*, she asked herself, once again second-guessing the snap decision to have him tag along to the island in the middle of the night. She was reminded of her many one-night stands and how awkward it was to get them out of the door the morning after. There was a reason she usually preferred they didn't spend the night. *He'll only be in the way today. I don't even know him. Oh, Anna. What have you done?*

In the kitchen, she readied the coffee brewer. Without a strong cup, she wouldn't be able to think straight. Then she called Sven.

"Are you up yet?" She tried to be funny.

"I am now," came his reply followed by a big yawn. "Jeez, Anna, it's not even seven o'clock in the morning. Couldn't you let me sleep in for a bit?"

"Don't you have a job to get to?"

"I do, but I usually sleep until seven-thirty. Besides, what's it to you?"

"I need your help today, looking for Pa."

"I had a hunch you'd say that, so I took a couple of days off. Let me get ready and I'll come over, okay? Breakfast's on you. I can't work on an empty stomach."

"Deal! And thank you!" Anna hung up. Breakfast she could do. She checked the fridge and found it well stocked with everything she needed. The pantry also provided an abundance of cereal, mueslis, and bread, sliced and stored in plastic bags, ready to toast. Even after more than a decade away, nothing had changed in her childhood home. She set the table, grabbed a cup of steaming hot coffee, and headed to the shower.

When she returned, Ali was sitting at the kitchen table, his eyes bloodshot and a steaming cup of coffee in front of him. He looked exhausted.

"Good morning." She smiled at him. "Did you get any sleep?"

"I did, but not nearly enough. You know, new bed and all the excitement."

"I do. Same here. I see you helped yourself to some coffee. Any good? I'm not used to my parents' old coffeemaker anymore."

"Yes, thank you. I just walked in. Haven't tasted it yet, but I'm sure it's great."

Anna considered the situation. Here she was with this stranger whom she'd known for what? Half a day? Yet their interaction was as domestic as could be. Weird. *You better not get used to that.* Better not think about it in the first place. She needed her wits about her and her mind focused on finding Pa. But how could she get rid of Ali? Politely, of course.

They drank their coffee in silence. The house lay quiet until Anna saw Sven arrive, riding his three-wheel flatbed moped, the traditional mode of transportation on all islands in the archipelago. It made her nostalgic as she remembered the countless times he'd shown up at their house, exactly like this, since he'd bought this very moped at the tender age of fifteen, having worked all summer on a fishing boat to earn enough to buy one and get the license to drive it legally. That was a different story entirely, especially on the islands, where laws were considered "written by mainlanders for mainlanders." Laws only applied sporadically out here, when it suited someone to invoke them to their advantage. Otherwise, they were up for debate.

Seconds later, Sven opened the front door, forgoing the doorbell or a knock, another weird island custom, especially among friends. Given it was early and most normal people would still be asleep, not knocking was not an unwise choice.

Having seen him arrive, Anna got up to greet him at the door and gestured him inside, telling him to keep it down as Tore was still asleep. "I made him take a sleeping pill last night. He needs to rest up."

"Good morning, Ali. Did you get any sleep?" Sven asked politely as he walked into the kitchen a step behind Anna. Ali tried to get up, but Sven gestured for him to stay seated, putting his hand on the man's shoulder. "No need to get up for me." He smiled, but there was sadness in his voice and all over his face.

Anna looked at her best friend, her "BFF" as they'd called each other growing up, unusual as it was for a girl and a boy to hang out and be so close without anything ever happening. At the time, Anna had made it clear she was a lesbian. Little did she know back then. Or was it just that she hadn't been into Sven? Looking at him now, she wondered why. He was a very handsome specimen for a male. Tall, towering at least six feet, with broad shoulders, and his short, blond hair and blue eyes would make him a catch in the eyes of most women. As far as she knew, he was straight; he'd had girlfriends off and on throughout their years in school, yet he was still single. It was unusual for someone their age to be unattached out here where everybody knew everyone and where there was a lid for virtually every pot. Alas, as of now, Sven seemed to have dodged any marriage proposals.

"Have you heard anything?" Sven asked.

"No. We're waiting for the police to return. According to Dad, they'll bring divers today. That just freaks me out! Why didn't they search overnight?" Anna began to set the breakfast table.

Sven shrugged. "I don't know. Maybe it's because they don't have the resources? With all the gang violence in town, the police are stretched pretty thin. I haven't seen a traffic patrol in over a decade. That says a lot. As for the divers, I guess it just makes no sense to go dive in the dark, does it?" He threw his arms in the air in a desperate gesture before grabbing a mug from the cupboard. He poured himself a cup of black coffee and joined Ali at the table.

Anna decided now was as good a time to call the police as any. She picked up the phone attached to the wall near the entrance to the kitchen and dialed the number of the police inspector in charge of the search. Her father had left his business card on the kitchen table.

"This is Peter Gustavson, Gothenburg police."

"Good morning. This is Anna Svensson. I'm calling about my father, Lennart Svensson."

"Ah, yes, Ms. Svensson. We're on our way. We expect to be there just before eight a.m. Is there anything I can do for you now?"

"What can you tell me about the search so far?"

"Not much. We did several helicopter sweeps of the islands yesterday after dark but couldn't detect anybody that wasn't just out for a walk. With all the people looking for your father, the forest was quite busy. But it was too dark to send out the divers. They're coming with me this morning. I hope to be able to send the helicopter out again today, too."

"Do you know when he disappeared? My father says after breakfast?"

Sven cut in. "That's not quite accurate. I came by yesterday after breakfast to see him. We were discussing a secret project for Tore. I already told the police about it. But I did leave just after ten."

"So you were the last one to see him alive?" Anna stared at Sven.

"I guess."

"We did speak to Sven Johansson yesterday," the inspector said, "and his alibi checks out."

"Alibi? Is he a suspect?"

"No, of course not. We treat this as a missing-person case. The most likely scenario is that your father fell and hurt himself. We will sweep the island again today with our dog patrols and also dive in a couple of places where he might have fallen into the water."

A yelp escaped Anna's throat as she contemplated the latter.

"This must all be upsetting. I am very sorry. Why don't we continue this conversation once I'm on the island? How is your father holding up?"

"He's upstairs. I gave him something to sleep."

***

Less than an hour later, three police officers arrived at the house. Tore was still asleep, and Anna didn't have the heart to disturb him. She went to the front door before they could ring the bell and accidentally wake him up.

"Good morning, Officers. Please come in." She gestured them inside and showed them the way to the kitchen.

"Good morning. My name is Police Inspector Peter Gustavson, and these are my colleagues. I guess you were the one who called me a while ago? We're in charge of helping you find your father." The inspector looked at the other two men in the kitchen and stretched out his hand to greet them. Anna made the introductions.

"Is your father awake? Can we speak to him?"

"He's still asleep. Is there anything you need from him right this instant? Or can I help you?" Anna wasn't sure what the inspector was looking for. She'd already given them all the information she had.

The inspector looked down at the floor, squirming, before he said, "In these cases, we find that the partner of the missing person often knows a lot more than they initially tell us. It's not unusual for them to be the reason the person went missing in the first place. We would like to speak to him again, see if he remembers anything else."

"So you're saying my dad killed my pa?"

"No, I didn't say that, although that is one possible explanation. For now, we can only hypothesize. There may have been a disagreement of sorts and your father left the house. That or maybe he fell ill somewhere out there, which is why we need to find him as soon as possible."

Anna gasped at the suggestion of Pa lying hurt out there in the cold and humid September night.

"Can you please get your father?" The inspector remained strangely calm. Anna nodded and went up to wake him up.

***

Tore was still groggy as Anna escorted him into the kitchen and was upset to see all the people in his house. Ali and the inspector were sitting at the kitchen table while Sven and two other officers were milling around in the background. Anna pulled out a chair for Tore and helped him sit down.

"Good morning, Mr. Svensson," the inspector began. "We would like to talk to you again. See if you remember anything else about yesterday."

Tore shook his head. "I'm sorry. This is all so very confusing. I don't understand. Lennart was his regular self, looking forward to getting out and going on his walk before he met his friends."

"Friends? You didn't mention he had plans to see friends."

"He often does. They meet up at Styrsö BK, our local sports club, to drink coffee and chat, or work on the hiking paths around the island. They meet up every week, but some of them can't get enough of it and meet up any day of the week."

"We'll look into that. Thank you. Where does he usually take his walks? Are there any places he visits more frequently? I'm also interested in places that are close to the water." The inspector laid out a map of the island on the kitchen table and asked Tore to point to potential places to search.

"Well, there's Brännholmsviken, of course. But that's so shallow I find it difficult to believe he'd be able to drown. The water's only inches deep near the beach, and I'm sure someone would've seen him there by now. But to the south of the bay, out by Gula Udden, there are cliffs he could theoretically have fallen off. The water is pretty deep, and few people walk out there. He has been known to spend time watching ships pass.

"Then there's Salskärs Headland, north of here. Again, not a place where people go often, but occasionally you'll see someone hike out there. Lennart tends to avoid the places where the tourists mill about, so those two places are the ones I'd go look at." Tears flowed down Tore's cheeks as he pictured Lennart sitting on those beautiful cliffs overlooking the sea.

"Thank you. That's very helpful." The inspector instructed his colleagues to relay the information to the dive team, and they left the room. "Let's go back to yesterday. Can you tell me what happened at the breakfast table?"

Tore looked at him curiously. It was the strangest question. "Nothing happened. It was just like every other day around here. We woke up. We made breakfast, ate together, read the papers, and then we got ready for the day, showered, and shaved. You know, what most retirees do. Lennart was still in the shower when I left. I had an appointment in the city and had to catch a ferry, so I couldn't join him for his walk. Not that I usually do. We've been together so long that we respect each other's need for alone time, and Lennart loves his walks. He's a Pathfinder with the local sports club."

"Pathfinder?" one of the officers asked. Tore hadn't noticed her return.

"Yes. About fifteen years ago, our local soccer club organized a group of older people to improve the hiking trails around the island. They got some money from the city, even some funds from the European Union. It was a big thing. They hauled hundreds of wheelbarrows of macadam into the forest to create this network of nature hikes. It's quite an accomplishment. The group calls itself Pathfinders, and they've been at it ever since. The trails require regular maintenance, plus they add a new stretch now and then. Lennart joined them when he retired from his job a few years ago. All of the members also love to hike, so they're often in the woods, alone or in groups."

"I see. I presume you've spoken to his friends?" the inspector asked. "They haven't heard from him?"

"Yes, I have, and we've already searched every path on the island. We did that yesterday, all afternoon and evening. Nothing."

"And you say his phone was left here at the house?"

"Yes, he left it on his nightstand. We talked about this yesterday, didn't we? It's still where he left it. That's not unusual for him. He's not the most IT-savvy person and never cared much for gadgets, which is odd, given that he's an engineer."

"We'll most likely need that phone for technical analysis at some point. You never know what you can find on these devices. But not yet." The inspector tried again. "Was there anything unusual about yesterday? Did you fight or argue about something? Or maybe the night before? Was there anything that you can think of that could've prompted your husband to leave without saying a word?"

Tore began to cry and shook his head. "Honestly? I can't think of anything. We've been together for forty-nine years. Sure, we had our disagreements, but nothing of the sort that would cause him to leave me, and most certainly not without his phone or his wallet. It makes no sense. The past few days were normal, there was nothing out of the ordinary. No fights, no arguments, just your average weekend. We'd been in town shopping for new shoes for the upcoming season. That's it."

The inspector made notes. "Well, thank you for clarifying things again for us. And please, if you remember anything else, let us know immediately. Regardless of how inconsequential it may seem to you, any detail could be important."

The police then talked to Anna about Lennart, asking her about her relationship with her parents, potential reasons for fights, and things that might have upset Lennart enough to leave, but she was of no help. She didn't know enough about their lives these days, but Tore was relieved to hear her tell the inspector that if it was anything like the way it was when she'd still lived here, there was no way Pa would leave him. It was unfathomable. This had to have been an accident, and the fact that Lennart had been missing for almost a day already meant the chances of finding him alive were dwindling rapidly.

One of the officers also talked to Sven, and Tore was surprised to hear about the secret project Lennart had wanted Sven to work on for him, to turn the shed into a guest cabin for a small bed-and-breakfast.

"You came here at what time, did you say?" the inspector asked.

Tore was torn between despair and feeling all this love for his husband. He hugged Sven tightly. "You're probably the last person to see him alive before he left the house. You're my last connection to Lennart. Thank you, Sven! Thank you for everything."

Sven blushed and looked at Anna apologetically.

– 7 –

September 7, 2022

I<small>T TURNED OUT</small> to be a crazy day at the house. The police were coming and going, having established a sort of command center there from where they coordinated the continued search. Ali felt useless, but rather than asking Anna to take him to the harbor to take the next ferry into town, which he felt she didn't have time for, he busied himself around the house, making beds, cleaning bathrooms and the kitchen, making coffee and serving people, eventually making lunch for everybody.

Nobody appeared to notice that he wasn't a fixture of the house. Anna was too busy looking after her father, who was too busy worrying about his husband, and Sven was too busy helping the police coordinate the search, telling them where to look, showing them to various spots on the island where Lennart would usually walk, first on maps, later taking people there, rallying the islanders to help out, too. The police simply ignored Ali.

The entire island seemed to be engaged in looking for Lennart. Police dogs had arrived with their handlers, sniffing Lennart's clothes, then going off in a million directions, following scents so faint they were unavailable to humans. The canine searchers dashed off, and they covered the entire island.

It wasn't until late in the afternoon of this second day of searching for Lennart that Anna came into the kitchen and stopped dead in her tracks, watching Ali dry some dishes and put them away. "You're still here?" She seemed horrified.

He merely shrugged.

"But don't you need to get back to work? I'm so sorry. I've been so busy, I completely forgot about you."

"It's okay. It's all taken care of. I can stay a little longer if that's okay with you. Although I need to look into the whole parking situation at some point."

"Fuck. Let me talk to Sven. Maybe we can move your car to another rented parking. There's always someone who's away for a few days." She pulled her phone from her back pocket and sent a quick text. "I feel awful about doing this to you. This was certainly not what you signed up for." She smiled at him gratefully. "And here you are, doing dishes." As if yet another realization dawned upon her, her mouth fell open and her hands flew to her cheeks. "You cooked, too, didn't you? Oh my God! I am so, so sorry. I completely missed that. I just kind of came in here, sat down, and ate. I should've known the food was way too good to have been cooked by Dad. Pa was always the cook in our family. Thank you so much!" She crossed the distance and spontaneously hugged Ali. "You're a gem. How can I repay you? How much do I owe you?"

Still holding a plate and a towel, Ali waved his hands dismissively. "Don't mention it. I'm glad I can be of assistance. I couldn't have stuck around here and done nothing. And you've all been so busy with the search and everything. I wouldn't have found my way to the ferry." He blushed. "I figured it was better I got busy."

"I don't know what I was thinking." Anna was quickly losing it and began to cry. "I'm so sorry I did this to you, interrupting your life like this."

Ali put down the towel and the plate and gave her a long hug, whispering, "It's okay. I'm happy to help. Please don't feel bad on my account. This has been a good day for me, being able to be truly useful. The fact that you didn't notice me kind of proves my point. I have no family here in Sweden and very few friends. Trust me when I say this is good. It's been a good day, even though it has been difficult watching you and your father suffer. I wish I could do more, but I'd only be in the way in any effort to aid in the search."

Anna looked up into Ali's eyes as if trying to gauge his sincerity, then surprised him by suddenly moving in and kissing him. Ali recoiled slightly, but not in disgust.

"Are you sure you're doing this for the right reasons?"

Anna moved away from him. "I'm so sorry! I just...you have such lovely brown eyes, and you look so kind. I...I don't know what came over me. I feel so alone right now. Would you please just hold me?"

"Of course." Ali put his arms around her, one hand between her shoulder blades, the other on the small of her back, gently pulling her into his embrace as she began to sob. "It's okay, let it all out," he murmured. "I'm not going anywhere."

– 8 –

September 7, 2022

LATER IN THE afternoon, Sven came by to pick up Ali, and together they took his boat to Saltholmen. Ali's car needed to be moved. A neighbor, a friend of Sven's, was out of town, and they were allowed to borrow her parking spot for the next couple of days.

When they returned to the island, Sven was invited to stay for dinner. Ali had found some beef in the fridge and had prepared a roast in the oven with potatoes, carrots, and other vegetables. He'd left it simmering on the stove, having instructed Anna to add more liquid if needed.

"But I don't know the first thing about cooking!" she'd said.

Ali had laughed. "Just add a bit of red wine every twenty minutes and we'll be fine."

Upon his return, the stew was perfect. All he had to do was add a bit of salt and some Cayenne pepper to ensure it tasted the way he'd intended it to. Anna went to the living room to pick up her father, made sure Sven stayed put, and all four of them ate in silence, each busy with their thoughts and the lack of progress in the rescue effort.

The police were still searching the island, having received reinforcements from a helicopter that had previously been occupied elsewhere. As dusk descended, it began to circle above Styrsö again. With its heat camera, it might be able to find Lennart if he were lying somewhere, hurt and unable to move. Chances were slim, though. It was the second evening it had hovered out there, above the island, searching. They hadn't found anything the evening before, so why now? Styrsö was, after all, not that big, and virtually the entire island population had been out looking for Lennart all day. Even the local school had participated, walking every path on the island. Members of the Pathfinders were also out and about again, looking for their missing friend. Alas, not a trace of Lennart.

The police dogs had picked up his scent all over the island, leading away from the house. Throughout the day, the dog teams had walked through the forest and crisscrossed the entire island, but to no avail. One dog had taken them to Lennart's favorite spot, about a twenty-minute walk from the house, at Salskärs headland, where visitors and locals alike could, if they chose, enjoy unparalleled views of the Gothenburg harbor inlet, the open sea westward, the cargo vessels anchoring as they awaited their turn to offload or load their cargo, and in the distance, the lighthouse of Vinga with its pyramid-shaped large beacon. However, it was out of the way for most visitors, and locals had other spots they preferred, which was why it had always been Lennart's favorite place.

The police eventually began to focus on the theory that he may have slipped on a rock or had a stroke or heart attack and fallen into the water. The strong currents would quickly drag a body away from the site. Police divers searched the area and used underwater robots but found no trace of him. They would continue their search for another day, but chances of finding Lennart alive were decreasing by the hour.

Peter Gustavson, the police inspector, summarized the search effort for Tore and Anna. Nothing was new to them, yet reading between the lines, Anna understood that hope was almost lost.

"We've been conducting interviews all day with people who were close to Lennart, but except for Sven here, nobody saw him yesterday. We've looked at his phone records, and there were no calls made to or from it. We will, of course, double-check with the phone company's official records, but as we don't suspect any crime, this is just a routine check.

"The dogs are done with their work, and the divers have spent a lot of time around Salskärs Udde, to no avail as you know.

Tomorrow, they'll be on the other side of the island, just to make sure. The dogs did not pick up any strong scent so this is more to make sure than anything else. I'm afraid to say I don't expect us to find him there.

"Based on what we've been able to put together from what you've told us—which has been corroborated by your friends and neighbors—Lennart most likely took a stroll to Salskärs Udde after leaving the house, slipped somehow, fell into the water, and drowned. The tidal currents would have moved his body away from the island, given the time of day. I'm sorry we don't have better news for you.

"The investigation will be handed over to our Missing Persons Unit. That's routine. They'll be in touch with you, but from an investigative point of view, there is very little they'll be able to do. They'll double-check the phone records once they're in, but as I said, there's no suspicion of a crime, and in time, they'll close the investigation, which will be important to you, as a family. It'll allow you to have him declared legally dead and move on with your lives. I'm sorry. I understand that's not what you hoped to hear."

He left the house shortly afterward, and for a moment, silence reigned around the kitchen table. It was Anna who spoke first.

"I think I'll head home tomorrow. There's nothing I can do here anyway, and I have to get back to work."

Tore looked at her and nodded, a broken man. She couldn't imagine how he felt inside, the loss that must be weighing him down, tearing him apart from the inside out. On the other hand, she also couldn't bring herself to care, which hurt her almost more than the loss of her father. She and Dad had been at loggerheads for decades, and while she loved him, she didn't like him very much. She often felt their relationship had been the model upon which Facebook defined its "complicated" box. Yet she felt conflicted, guilty. Would she be abandoning her father? What would others say? Would the island forgive her? Judge her? Damn her? If they did, it wouldn't be the first time. Anna had decided years ago to no longer give a damn what Styrsö thought about her and her life choices. She wasn't about to renege on that decision, as difficult as it was right at this moment.

Tore went to bed shortly after dinner, while Sven stayed behind to help with the dishes.

"That's not necessary," Anna stopped him. "We can manage."

"Are you sure? I'm happy to help."

"I know, I know. But you've done so much already, and I'm sure you have a life to get back to, especially since you've been here all day, helping with the search. Thank you so much." She hugged him but gently pushed him out of the kitchen.

Sven took the hint, looked over her shoulder at Ali, and thanked him for dinner. "It was delicious!" He hugged Anna and left. "I'll text you tomorrow to see if you need anything. Okay?" He must've felt bad he was unable to do more for her, a futile emotion Anna couldn't reciprocate.

When she came back into the kitchen, Ali had already begun doing the dishes. She joined him, grabbing a towel. They didn't speak much, and work flowed quickly as they established a natural routine. They were done in no time.

"Do you want some coffee?" Ali asked.

Anna smiled. "Isn't that my job to offer my guest?"

Ali shrugged. "Well, I do. Do you want a cup, too?" He was already moving toward the pantry to pick up the coffee.

"Yeah, I'll join you." Anna sat at the kitchen table and watched Ali go through the motions of making coffee; within minutes, the entire space was filled with the familiar and comforting aroma. Anna got up and collected a bottle of wine from the pantry.

"I think I'll need a glass later on. Join me?"

Ali didn't answer right away, as he was busy pouring the coffee into two mugs. "Oh, I'm sorry. I forgot you're Muslim. Are you even allowed to drink?"

Ali laughed. "Yes, I am a Muslim, and yes, I do drink. I've never been very religious—you could call me agnostic. I love a good glass of wine, but I'm not partial to pork. So here you go, I'm your typical secular Muslim. I don't fast either, but I do celebrate Eid." He shrugged, smiling crookedly. "Is that okay for you?"

"Whatever floats your boat! Same here, although I am partial to bacon. I'm not a member of any congregation either. Totally secular family. My fathers brought me up as an atheist, and I never had a reason to question that. I do respect other people's beliefs, though, even if I can't understand why anyone would choose fantasy over science." Anna picked up the bottle opener and pulled the cork out of the bottle's neck. She smelled the tip of the cork before throwing it into the trash. Pouring herself a little bit of wine into a glass to taste it, she sat down again.

"When do you have to go back to Stockholm?" she asked.

"I should probably leave tomorrow when you leave. My friend needs the car. Without it, he can't make money, and neither can I. But I'll stay as long as you need me to."

"I don't want to keep you here—no, that came out wrong." She took a deep breath before continuing. "I'm very grateful to you and for the help you've provided today. But I can't ask that you stay, especially not after I'm gone. That would be completely inappropriate."

"But your father? Will he be okay on his own?"

"No, of course not. He also won't be okay if I stay. We'd fight again before long, and it would make things even worse. Eventually, one of us will say something the other will regret. Dad and I are at our best from a distance." She smiled weakly and shrugged. "But will you be okay? I worry about you, which is weird. I mean, seriously, we've known each other for how long? A day? Yet I feel as if I've always known you. It's such a strange thing, and all the while, we go through this crisis with my missing father. I honestly don't know what's what anymore. I'm not even sure if my words make any sense." She put her hand on his. "You have this calming effect on me. You, a complete stranger. I think I'm going crazy. That's it. I'm losing it."

"Don't worry. I think it's a natural, protective instinct in times of crisis, and I understand what you're going through. At the beginning of the civil war in my country, my favorite uncle disappeared. We never heard what happened. One day, he went to the market and never returned. Chances are he was picked up by the GID. We don't know. It was as if he was swallowed by the Earth. Same thing with my father and my brothers. Simply gone. I'm sure they would have picked me up as well if I'd stayed in Aleppo." He shrugged. "But I'm glad if I have a calming effect on you. I certainly don't feel very calm within."

"Whatever it is you do, keep it up." Anna picked up her phone and turned it back on. "Maybe I should check messages from work and get back in the saddle. As you know, we have an election coming up this weekend, and one of my clients is a political party running for government."

As soon as her work line connected to the grid, it started beeping and making all kinds of strange noises.

"Shit! Shit, shit, shit!" Anna exclaimed as she read the notifications of countless texts and missed calls. She must have missed something major at work. She read the texts from Anders, her boss. "Fuck! There's been a scandal in Stockholm. It's all over the tabloids and Twitter. I haven't even looked at the news today. Please excuse me, I need to go and deal with this." Grabbing her glass of wine, she got up and disappeared into her room.

– 9 –

September 7, 2022

Look, Anders, I understand. I'll fly back in the morning. It's too late now, and I'm not pulling another all-nighter."

"Understood. So what's your take? What should we do?" The question sounded raspy through Anna's headphones.

"I think they need to own it. Be honest about it. Apologize. Tell the whole story. I mean, the original article is skewed toward his wife's point of view. Acknowledge, apologize, explain, and contextualize. If they stay quiet, it'll be like oxygen to the flame, making this much bigger than it needs to be. The tabloids are having a field day. The Americans would talk about this being an October surprise. We need to put a lid on it."

"Makes sense, but are you sure an apology is the way to go in this instance?"

"Yes! Absolutely. Because if he doesn't, the opposition is going to run with it, not to mention that women, who are a main voting demographic of theirs, aren't normally as forgiving of adultery as men might be. However, if he apologizes sincerely and then gives some context, the story might die by itself. It's not like this is something that hasn't happened to others. Half of Sweden's marriages end in divorce. They're just being human, and I think a lot of people will relate to that. But we also have to consider those who aren't involved, those outside the limelight, his wife, and the kids. The last thing you want is cameras outside their homes. That would make it worse, and I believe people would start to place blame on the party for not handling it appropriately."

Anders seemed to be contemplating his response. "Yeah, I can see how that would be unfortunate. So you're coming home tomorrow?"

Anna sighed. "Yes. Pa is still missing, but the way things look right now, they're not going to find him. The police say he's most likely fallen into the ocean and drowned. There's not much I can do here, and Dad is just annoying me with his looks and his innuendo. I can stay in touch by phone. This place is creeping me out right now."

"Excellent. I'll see you in the office then. And you will send a draft press release within the hour?"

"Yes, boss. I will."

They hung up, and Anna pulled out her laptop to write the press release. This was exactly why she didn't do relationships. Inevitably, they ended up in chaos and led to broken hearts. She pitied the wife of the party chairman who'd been caught with his pants down. Worse still, it had happened with someone who worked for him, a political secretary, young and pretty. The optics were anything but good, especially with the wife and her two young kids, and Anna knew that if the press started hounding the wife for comments, things would get out of hand and the party would take a beating at the polls. They would anyway, as a large segment of the party's voters were women who took infidelity seriously, but they might still steer clear of the worst by reclaiming the narrative. Anna hated this aspect of her job, cleaning up the mess others made. She vowed right there and then never to fall for anyone romantically, to avoid the messiness of the inevitable breakup. The thought was pushed aside by the image of Ali sitting at her father's kitchen table. She let out a deep sigh. *Not helping.*

After she'd written the press release and sent it to her boss and the client, she went downstairs to make sure the lights were out. It had taken a long time, yet Ali was still sitting by the kitchen table.

"What are you still doing up?"

"Not much. Just sitting here, contemplating things, catching up on news." He showed her his phone screen, displaying the front page of one of Sweden's tabloid newspapers. "So this is your client?"

Anna nodded. "Yeah, it's a mess, too, as you can see. The tabloids love this stuff. Sells their garbage more easily."

Ali put his phone down and looked at her. "So what are you going to do? In my country, this person would be toast."

"Well, they're going to take a beating at the polls, that's for sure. But if we handle it right, with a large dose of humility, maybe we can avoid the worst and they won't fall below the four-percent line and have to leave parliament. My client relies largely on a female base, and they're not exactly going to condone his behavior. They stand to lose at least a percentage point or two, which is a lot for a party their size." She shrugged. "Men! Why can't they keep their dicks under control?" Ali shrank in his chair, blushing. "Sorry, present company excluded. I didn't mean to—"

Ali put up a hand. "I didn't think you did. Look, it's been a long day. I'll head to bed if that is okay with you, and tomorrow I'll head back to Stockholm. Be out of your hair."

"Yeah, me, too. Unfortunately, I'll have to fly home. I've already booked the flight, as I need to be in the office as soon as possible. I hope you'll forgive me."

"Yeah, of course. You don't owe me anything. You've paid for your trip already, and besides, I owe you and your father for your generosity and hospitality."

Anna laughed. "Are you for real? It is we who owe you, for everything you've done here today."

"Would you mind if I asked for your number? Just so I can check up on you in a few days to make sure everything's okay?"

"Yeah, sure." They exchanged numbers and then they went to bed.

– 10 –

September 8, 2022

ANNA AND ALI left Styrsö early in the morning on the 5:39 ferry from Bratten. Anna had booked herself on an early flight from Landvetter, and Ali was driving her to the airport, as it was on his way home. She'd be landing at Bromma Airport within an hour while he'd spend another five hours on the road. Anna knew that he'd rather have her by his side for the trip home, but she needed to be in Stockholm as quickly as possible to deal with the situation brewing there. Anders and the party secretary had scheduled a meeting for nine o'clock, which was the earliest possible given her flight schedule, to discuss the scandal with the party officials and agree on the next steps.

Ali stopped the car outside the terminal, and Anna got out, but before she closed the door, she looked back to thank him, shaking her head. The sight of him behind the wheel made her want to cry. *Why?* She closed the door and abruptly turned and walked away. She'd have to apologize for her behavior later, but she had to focus on herself now, on work, yet as she entered the terminal, she wondered if Ali was still parked by the curb, watching her, or if he'd already left. The thought flashed through her mind that she could abandon her flight and join him for the trip back north, but she quickly pushed it away. *Get a grip! You have work to do.*

The flight was short and on time. The man next to her was reading *Dagens Industri*, Sweden's daily economic newspaper, and the headlines made it clear the scandal had reached the morning papers.

The passenger saw her looking at his paper and shook his head. "This is going to be the end of them. There's no way they can recover from this. Not a day too soon, either, what with their extremist policies." He added several colorful expletives.

Anna didn't comment. It was no surprise that her client wasn't popular in business circles. Her own political beliefs didn't fully line up with those of her client either, but she was committed to making sure the party didn't suffer because of one man's unruly penis. It wouldn't be easy. While most people understood infidelity and that there were a great many reasons why people acted the way they did and betrayed their partners, voters often showed a more rigid moral compass when it came to the politicians representing them, and even more so toward those whose political convictions they didn't share. For a small party, that spelled a lot of trouble. They might more easily forgive their partners for their infidelity than politicians...which gave her an idea. She had to make sure to disassociate the man from the party and frame his actions even more as those of a man, not a politician. But how? And would it work?

Arriving in Stockholm, she rushed out of the terminal to grab a taxi to take her to the meeting on Kungsgatan. Luckily, it didn't take more than twenty minutes to get there, giving her a few minutes to freshen up and prepare.

The meeting itself was tense. The party chair was still in shock, moving from a state of denial to random accusations, feeling betrayed by how the news of his infidelity had leaked, blaming his mistress at times, then the journalist who had leaked it—someone he knew, of course—worrying about his career, the damage to his marriage, his kids. They spent the better part of the first half hour just trying to calm him down, getting him to see reason, and keep a level head. It wasn't easy.

After that, things moved quickly, as an emergency meeting with the party leadership, which had convened overnight without his knowledge or presence, made things easy for him by asking him to resign immediately. This was sort of what Anna had in mind, although her idea had been for him to step aside temporarily. Alas, neither party nor voters had any confidence left in him; snap polls conducted overnight had cast a damaging light, and the events were risking the party's future in the Swedish Riksdag. In the end, he had no choice, and a short press conference was called, where his resignation was announced. His deputy, a young woman with Persian roots, had to step up, just days before the election, a day before the big debate on TV4, and only forty-eight hours before the final public debate on Swedish National Television. Prepping her was now the only priority for the party, to avoid complete obliteration.

It was Anna's task to make sure the deputy was prepared, not from a political perspective, the party would see to that, but providing her with an adequate narrative as someone cast into the limelight against all odds. Anna and the team hoped that the sympathy vote would prove strong enough to keep the party in parliament. They wouldn't know until Friday when additional polls would provide some insights.

By the time Anna came back to her apartment that night, darkness had long ago fallen across the city. Outside, she found a bag with the food delivery from two nights ago. She picked it up, grossed out that they'd just left it there, and threw it in the trash without opening it. She had lost her appetite and didn't order anything else. She turned on her private line, and it beeped three times. There was a message from Dad, one from Ali, and one from Sven. Her dad informed her that the police had called off the search after not finding anything today either, as they had suspected, and he included the contact info for the Missing Persons Unit at the Gothenburg police division, which would take over the case now.

Sven's message was short but to the same effect. He once again reiterated that he'd be there for her. While she didn't reply to her father, unsure what to say, she sent a quick message to Sven, acknowledging the news and thanking him for keeping an eye on Tore.

She'd saved Ali's message for last but was disappointed—*why?*—when it was just a short message letting her know that he'd safely returned to Stockholm. Nothing about how he was doing, not asking her about her day or anything. *Strange. Oh well, I guess he's moving on.* But why did this bother her? Why had she hoped for more?

Exhausted from the past couple of days, Anna ran a bath and soaked for a long time, catching up on a TV show she was following. All the while, she couldn't stop thinking about Ali. Why had he not said anything about how his journey had been? Why had he not asked how she was doing? Was he upset with her? Had she done something wrong? As these questions flooded her consciousness, another side of her struggled with why she was having these thoughts. *He's a fucking Uber driver, not a date. Just forget him, move on. Maybe order some food after all? You might get lucky with the delivery guy.* She tried to picture the handsome Somali man standing at her door, but the image was supplanted by Ali's brown eyes and thick eyebrows. She relented and sent him a text.

> *Hey, Anna here. Glad you're back in town in one piece. Did everything go okay?*

She added *miss you!* but deleted that again and pressed send. *What's come over me? What am I doing?*

She had to wait longer than expected before her phone beeped and a notification of his response appeared on her screen. She opened it and read.

> *Sorry, I've been working all day, ever since I came home. Need to make up for time lost. It's crazy busy here. Can I call you tomorrow?*

– 11 –

September 11, 2022

Two days had come and gone. There had been no call from Ali, but Anna's job kept her so busy that she almost forgot to even think about him.

Friday night arrived, and she accompanied the interim party chair to Swedish National Television and their final debate between all party chairs, the *pièce de résistance* of the entire campaign and the final chance to make a good impression on undecided voters. Anna felt they had prepared as well as they could and that they would do well, considering the circumstances. Given the rush of news in the final days, political journalists had left the details of the scandal to their gossip columnists and had moved on to meatier, political matters.

The snap polling the party had commissioned showed that the damage to their numbers had been mitigated by the quick, decisive change in leadership, and the debate was a success. Anna felt accomplished. Her job was done, and the new chair had performed well. Now it was up to voters to decide.

Anna barely remembered Saturday, a blur of final engagements with the client in Stockholm, Gothenburg, and Malmö. She only attended the one in Stockholm, not wanting to travel anymore for the time being.

On Sunday morning, she allowed herself to sleep in before walking to a nearby café for breakfast and on to the polling station to cast her vote. The weather was gorgeous and sunny, and Anna decided to go for a walk downtown. She took the subway to the old town and walked over to the royal castle and across Strömbron toward Kungsträgården.

She didn't get very far before she noticed a familiar figure sitting on a bench, enjoying the pale mid-September sun. Ali.

"Hey!" She stopped and smiled, positioning herself between Ali and the sun.

"Anna! What a coincidence. How are you? I've been thinking about you."

"You have? I must've missed that notification on my phone." She tried to be funny, but traces of hurt laced her words.

"I'm sorry." Ali looked like a chastised dog. "I wanted to call, but I heard the news about the scandal, and I remembered you mentioning it as we drove to the airport, and then I worked almost day and night. In between that and trying to let you get your job done, it just kind of got lost. How's Tore doing? Have you heard from him? The search? I'm sorry. I should've called." The words gushed from Ali's mouth like a waterfall and then suddenly dried up.

Anna shook her head. She hadn't heard anything and had avoided calling her dad. "I'm sorry. I have no reason to be mad at you or to have any sort of expectation of you to call me or even stay in touch in the first place. I'm quite angry at myself for caring, which in itself is not the nicest thing to say, come to think of it. Argh!" Her hands flew to her face as she responded almost the same way Ali had, a weird stream of subconscious rambling without any forethought. She realized as much and continued, more subdued. "Look, this—" she pointed at herself, drawing a large circle around her head with her arm "—just isn't me. Not normally. Then again, as you've seen firsthand, these past days have been anything but, quote-unquote, normal for me. May I buy you a coffee? It's kind of chilly out here."

Ali smiled up at her, even though she was sure she looked like a mad woman gesturing wildly. "Sure. Lead the way. You're lucky, if that's the right word, as I was about to get up and go home."

Anna led the way to a bakery slash café about a ten-minute walk away and closer to the station, where they found a table amidst the Sunday crowd. After getting their coffee and cake, they sat down to enjoy their *fika*, chatting, just like countless others around them.

"You say you've been working almost nonstop since returning?" Anna asked.

"Yeah. Let's just say the two days in Gothenburg were not exactly healthy for my economy. Life in Sweden isn't cheap."

"I'm so sorry about that. Is there anything I can do to help? It's my fault, after all, that you had to drive all the way down there and waste your time."

"It's okay. I'll be fine. But tell me. How are you doing? Have you spoken to Tore? How's he holding up? I can't even imagine the pain of losing one's partner and not even getting the closure of having a body to bury. He must be completely devastated."

Hearing Ali speak the way he did about Dad, Anna instantly regretted that she'd not been in touch. Why did she so easily fall into the old rut? Wasn't she an adult who could break free, change, and do things differently? Blushing crimson red, she admitted as much in her head but said something else entirely, mostly to make herself feel better. "It's been crazy busy at work. I haven't even had the time to check in with him. I'll have to call him later."

Ali saw through the pretense. "But you're here, walking through town? Clearly you—"

She threw her hands in the air in exasperation, interrupting him. "I know, I know. I put it off. I'm a bad daughter, a miserable human being. There, I said it."

"Please, Anna, that is not what I was trying to say. You and your father have some issues to work through, but you lost a parent and he lost his husband. You both know what it's like to have unfinished business. Do you want that to happen with Tore?"

"No, of course not. But you can't imagine what it was like growing up with him."

"I don't presume to know. What I do know is that even if your father is a failure, and mine was for sure, it's an entirely different proposition to suddenly face the fact that he's gone and you've missed that last chance to tell him you love him, regardless. I often think about that lost opportunity, the countless chances I let pass me by, to tell my father how I felt. Instead, I took him and his shortcomings for granted."

"You're right. Of course you're right!" Anna smiled at him. "I certainly recognize the reluctance that keeps me from taking that first step, particularly in the light of his stubbornness."

Ali laughed. "I think that's a trait you inherited from him."

Anna laughed, too. After that, they sat for a while in silence. Anna watched all the coming and going, the long queue at the counter behind Ali, where people were making their choices among the many delicious cakes, patisseries, and other baked goods.

"You never told me what happened between you and your father," Ali said, waking her from her daydreaming. "That is, if you're willing to talk about it."

"How much time do you have?"

Ali put up his hands. "How much time do you need?"

"Well, to give you context, I have to go all the way back to when my fathers met. That was a very different time. Both of them grew up on the island, and we're talking about the sixties and seventies. While Sweden was a progressive society in all kinds of ways, even back then, the islands were not. At least, not underneath a thin veneer. Being gay was frowned upon, and every gay child who was born out there eventually left and fled to the city. I know of kids who ended up on the other side of the planet just to get away from all the bullying and incessant persecution.

"In a way, my dads were super brave to stay put, even though they also moved to the city for a while. It wasn't until after I was born and my grandparents had passed away that they moved back to Styrsö, to the house they inherited. This was a time when they were not able to get married or adopt a child. I am Pa's biological daughter, and Dad wasn't able to adopt me until 2003. By then, I was already an adult, and we ran into a ton of legal issues.

That alone would have been enough to cause friction, but our history went way back to when I was a child."

Anna took a deep sigh before continuing. "Here's the thing. When my parents were young, they were ostracized by society, and even after the three of us moved back to the island in 1985, there were a lot of people who very vocally opposed their presence and me living with them. They were reported to social services, and it was an extremely stressful time for both of them. I don't think anyone can understand how difficult their situation was.

"To make matters worse, their relationship, while always loving, was deeply unequal. I was Pa's daughter, the house belonged to Pa, and there was no legal protection for them until our common laws changed in 1988. Not to mention the AIDS crisis, which affected a lot of people at the time. My parents were in a stable, monogamous relationship, but that didn't stop people from making assumptions, especially in the first years before society at large learned about how HIV was transmitted.

"I grew up amid all that, in a loving home, but I often felt as if I was walking on eggshells, and Dad in particular was super-conscious of every step I took, especially if it was slightly non-traditional. If I got bad grades, he worried that people would draw conclusions about their parenting. If I had a fight with a classmate, he feared social services would call on us again. My clothes, my makeup, my choice of friends—everything about me was constantly viewed through the lens of 'what is Styrsö going to think?'

"The fact that he was home only every few months and then almost twenty-four seven for weeks on end made it even more difficult. He wanted to be a part of my life, then left for months. When he came back, he expected us to go back to the way things had been, even though I had gone through significant personal development while he was away. It was easier for other kids who had sailors as parents. Those men usually left the raising to their wives, but Dad wanted to play an active role. For whatever reason, we just always clashed."

Ali looked at her incredulously. "Wow. How did you cope with all that?"

"By making my parents' life a complete nightmare. I rebelled. I wore the shortest skirts and the most revealing tees, and I did pretty much everything I wasn't supposed to. I was also a total tomboy in a way. Most of my friends were male, and Sven has been my best friend for as long as I can remember. He always had a crush on me, but growing up, I strongly felt that relationships, regardless of what gender the person was, wouldn't be for me. I knew I'd be better off on my own.

"I sometimes wonder if that inability to love, romantically, was a choice or if I am truly aromantic. Mind you, me saying this as a queer woman is controversial at best, but yeah, here we are. Once I was old enough and started high school in the city, I had sex with boys and girls—another thing that drove my parents crazy. Pa was more relaxed about it all, but poor Dad, he was always so conscious about the inequality of our family constellation that he tried quite forcefully to mold me into the perfect daughter, and I never managed to live up to his fantasies."

"I am very sorry to hear that. Tore seems like the gentlest soul."

"Oh, don't get me wrong. He is a super-nice person—with everybody but me. I know he loves me and that he would do anything for me, but the dreams he had for me don't coincide with who I became. He's been disappointed in every single choice I've made in my life. Moving away from home so early, moving to Stockholm to study, my sexuality, my romantic interests, or rather lack thereof, the fact that he will never have grandchildren. The list goes on and on and on."

"Yeah, the grandkids..." Ali shook his head. "I get that from my mom, too. Even though she already is a grandmother, multiple times over, she still pressures me to get married and settle down."

"Right? As if it's some God-given right for parents to expect grandchildren." Anna shook her head.

"Well, maybe it's biology. Or maybe they just want us to experience the joy children bring to life the way they did?"

"Possibly. Would you want children? If you could? Sorry, that came out wrong. I mean if you were married."

"Yeah, I guess. I haven't thought about it in recent years. I felt I was too young before I left Aleppo, and since then, it's not been on my radar. I wouldn't even be able to provide for a wife."

"Aww, you're cute. But we're not living in the Middle Ages. In this country, both partners go to work and provide for each other, each based on their abilities."

"Yeah, yeah, make fun of me, but you're right. It was a lot easier to take the boy out of Syria than removing Syria from the boy." Ali blushed.

"I'm sure you'll meet a great woman soon enough. You're still young."

"I'll be forty next year. I'd hardly call that young, certainly not by Middle Eastern standards. My brothers were all married by the time they were twenty-five. I have nephews who are looking for brides." He seemed genuinely saddened by this, and Anna put her hand on his.

"Please, Ali, don't worry. While I may be past my childbearing prime and pregnancy could be risky at my age, getting married at our age is not unusual. Not at all. But you're right. You need to feel comfortable in your skin and feel good about your personal life, your finances, and so on before you consider making a serious commitment. It's not that women are looking for a rich guy to marry, at least, most of us aren't, but I think we still expect our partner to lead a stable life before we take that leap. If that makes any sense?"

"I guess. As I said, I haven't thought about this for years, but let me ask you this. Did Tore get to adopt you in the end?"

"Yes, he did. I mean, it was weird. I never considered him anything other than my father, but we did it for legal reasons, to provide all of us with a framework for the future. We played

71

through many what-ifs, and we decided it was important for us to have that stability in place, to avoid any problems."

"Such as?"

"Well, for one, Pa is five years Dad's senior. Let's assume, for the sake of the argument, that he was dead, and I got seriously ill. Without the adoption, Dad might not be allowed to visit me in a hospital or make decisions on my behalf. Then there's inheritance laws and whatnot, but I also believe it was important for Dad to finally become my true father, you know? After what I put him through as a child, all the sacrifices he made, everything he suffered, it made our relationship even more fragile, if that's possible, knowing I could just turn him away."

"But you didn't."

Anna smiled. "No, I didn't. I love both my parents."

"It's none of my business, but after what you've told me, I think you need to tell Tore how you feel. He must feel lonely now that he's all alone."

"You're wise beyond your years, you know that, right?" Anna looked Ali straight in the eyes and held his hand tightly.

"May I ask you something else?" he asked cautiously, stroking the back of her hand with his thumb. "What am I to you?"

The way he looked at her almost made Anna's heart jump out of her chest, and she felt as if she'd been cast as the lead in a cheesy rom-com. Everything about the situation screamed "Get out!" at her, yet for whatever reason, she felt perfectly calm and at ease, right here, sitting across from the man who'd just asked her the most consequential question she'd heard in years.

"Honestly? I'm not sure, but right now I want you to keep doing what you're doing and never stop. Is that a good enough answer?"

They both looked down at Ali's thumb stroking the back of Anna's hand. After a short while, he pulled her hand to his lips and kissed it, and she looked up at him and smiled.

"Wanna get out of here?"

– 12 –

September 11, 2022

"D AD? HOW ARE you?" Lying in bed, hunkered up against Ali's shoulder with his arm around her, Anna had finally decided to call Tore.

"I'm okay, dear, I'm okay. I get up in the morning, and I spend my days looking for Lennart. What else can I do? Unlike some, I'm not quite ready to give up on him."

Hearing his voice, how broken he was, ripped her apart. "I'm so sorry, Dad. I know how hard this is for you, and I wish I could tell you Pa's coming back, but you know I can't."

"I know, dear. It's fine. You be you and allow me to be me. Intellectually, I know you and the police are probably right. He fell into the water and drowned. But until I see his body, there's a part of me that can't accept that. Not yet. Forty-nine years, dear. He deserves that I hold on to him just a little longer, you know? That I don't give up hope. But tell me, how are you? Did you manage to resolve the crisis? I heard the news about your client."

"Yeah, what a nightmare. I think they made the right decisions, and Shirin did fine in the two final debates. We'll just have to see what the outcome of the election will be. Did you vote?"

"Yes, dear, this morning after breakfast. You don't think I'd forgo my civic duties, do you?"

"Well, you certainly would have a reason not to."

"No, no. It's okay. People are nice, and everybody at the polling station was most kind, helping me today."

"Are you eating?"

"I am, don't worry. I'm just not very hungry."

"Do I have to call Sven? Do you need anything?"

"No, dear. Konsum is just across the hill. It's a fifteen-minute walk. I can manage. I have my little Trolley Dolly with me, and I take it slow and easy."

"You will let me know if you need anything, right? I'm only a phone call away."

"Yes, dear, I know. But it's not just me who's lost someone. How are you holding up?"

"I'm okay. I guess I've been lucky to be able to focus on work these past couple of days. I'm sure it will sink in eventually. And I'm not alone. Which feels nice."

"Oh?" Anna heard the curiosity in Tore's tone.

"Ali's here with me," she said, peering up at the man sitting with his back against the headboard of her large bed.

"Ali? The young man who drove you here?" It sounded like Tore wanted to add something to that, but he didn't.

"Yeah, that's the one." She met Ali's gaze as she continued to speak. "I don't know. There's this connection, you know? I can't quite put my finger on it, but there was definitely chemistry, and then we accidentally ran into each other today. He's here with me."

"Well then, say hello from me, will you? And promise me to be careful."

Again, Anna had the sense that Tore wanted to say more but refrained from doing so. Whatever truce they were observing was fragile and could've been ruined by one wrong word. Was he judging her? No. His voice wasn't loud enough for that. Was he hopeful? Possibly. She wasn't sure. Maybe he was truly a broken man, his determination in tatters after the events of the week.

She passed on the message. "Dad says hi."

Ali smiled. "Give him my best."

"Ali says hi back," she said, and there was an awkward silence on the line for a moment. Maybe Tore was more self-conscious now he knew Anna was in his company. "Dad?"

"Yes?"

"You do know that I love you, right?"

She heard him exhale before he replied. "I know, dear. I love you, too."

She hung up.

Ali was right. She needed to repair their relationship. He was the only family she had left, and if this thing with Ali, whatever it was, didn't work out, it would be up to Dad to pick up the pieces and put her back together. Because whatever *this* was, it was the closest thing to a relationship she had ever had, and it scared her. The girl who didn't do relationships was suddenly falling for someone, hard and fast, and she enjoyed the sensation of it.

***

Later that night, after Ali had gone out to get some groceries to make dinner, they watched the election reporting on TV together. The first exit polls showed that there would be a change in government. Anna's client hadn't performed as well as earlier polls indicated, but given the scandal, they'd done okay and would remain in parliament. Seconds after the first exit poll had been released, Anna's phone rang.

"Good evening, Anders! Looks like they made it."

"Yes, and you played a major part in it all. The way you handled yourself these past days is quite remarkable. We're about to head down to their election party. Will you join us? I'm sure Shirin and her team will be most grateful to you." Her boss seemed giddy, not surprisingly, given how grim things had been just days ago. An election disaster would not have looked good on the company's resumé. This was their first political client, and success was vital if they wanted to grow this aspect of the firm's business.

"Let me think about it. Would it be okay if I bring a plus-one?"

"Of course! The more the merrier. I doubt Shirin will notice." Anders hung up.

Ali gave her a puzzled look.

"Fancy going to the post-election party?" she asked.

"I don't think I have clothes to wear to a party."

"Don't worry. They're very laid-back. T-shirts and jeans are their uniform. You'll fit right in. I'll just go and clean up real quick. It'll be fun, and I think we deserve this."

"As long as we don't stay too late. I have to work in the morning."

Anna kissed him. "That makes two of us."

– 13 –

September 15, 2022

THE UNEXPECTED CALL from Anna had been like balm for Tore's troubled soul, and when she'd told him she loved him, he'd barely known how to respond. Those words had not exactly been common between them over the years, and the older Anna had gotten, the less they'd been spoken.

Tore blamed himself. He hadn't been a very good father. He'd tried too hard, way too hard. Rather than embracing her, protecting her, he'd wanted to prepare her, toughen her ahead of the countless trials she'd face in this cruel and heartless world. All it had done was push her farther and farther away. His job hadn't helped. Being a sailor on a merchant vessel, he would be gone for months at a time, leaving raising Anna to Lennart. When he returned home, he would try to make up for lost time. He hadn't realized until it was too late that it had created a lot of uncertainty for her, one set of rules when she and Lennart were home alone and a completely different set when Tore was home from his tours.

There had been countless discussions, often heated, between him and Lennart when Anna was little. Not once had Lennart played the "she's mine" card or made him feel as if his word counted for less. Never. But they often disagreed, and in the end, their approach to raising their daughter, their only child, had been very inconsistent, with each father applying his own parenting ideology, leaving Anna in a state of parental dissonance. More often than not, she'd avoided them, retreated into her own world, and slowly but surely distanced herself from both of them.

It was no surprise when she moved out after high school and never returned. It had little impact at the time, as she'd barely been home the last few years. The gaping hole she'd left had already been filled with other engagements, things they did to try to overcome the emptiness. After retirement, Lennart began working more and more with his Pathfinder friends and immersed himself in working on the island trails, going all in. Tore was still working away, and by the time he retired and came home for good, Lennart was a busy man, which was when the idea of setting up a tiny bed-and-breakfast had first begun to form. However, Tore was useless with a hammer and nails and nothing came of his plans. He'd had no idea that Lennart was actively pursuing it on his behalf.

He felt such guilt for pushing Anna away, and now Lennart was gone and they were both alone. He'd need to try harder to find a way to make peace with her, his only child. He'd gladly give his life for her, without thinking about it, and he had always been proud of her for every step she'd taken to prevail despite his botched attempts at protecting her from a cruel, heteronormative society. He'd cried himself to sleep the night she'd told them she was queer. She'd have to endure so much pain, and he would be unable to protect, to shield her from it. Yes, part of him also knew he'd likely not see grandkids. That was before society had quickly and largely accepted rainbow families and embraced various forms of co-parenting. All around them, people were creating new forms of families: some kids even grew up with four parents, two moms and two dads, while others found exciting ways to make their dream of raising kids come true. The world was slowly changing for the better.

Tore thought back to how they had become parents, quite unexpectedly. When Lennart returned from Denmark with Anna, Tore's first reaction had been one of shock. While he had known Lennart had traveled there to help his sister, they hadn't discussed him taking on the role of a father. Parenting hadn't even been on the radar. A gay couple couldn't raise a child; that was the general tenor in society. It was, after all, 1981, but they managed, somehow. With Lennart's name on the birth certificate, there wasn't much the authorities could do. They hadn't been pleased, of course, and social services repeatedly paid them visits over the years after neighbors and other parties with a "vested interest" had reported them. Anger still boiled up within him at the thought. He felt even angrier at the fact that they had been right, in a way. Not that he and Lennart had been incompetent parents, but the fear of making mistakes, the fear of being ostracized had led him to raise Anna with a far too heavy hand, focusing so much more on appearances than simply loving the child. This wonderful, amazing daughter of theirs. It was a cruel irony that the perception of being unable to parent a child had given rise to his shortcomings as a father.

The thoughts of Anna hung over Tore like a dark cloud, and he decided he needed some fresh air. He got dressed and steered his slow and heavy steps toward Bratten. Maybe Öbergska was still open and he could go in for a beer, meet some of his neighbors for a chat and be a little less lonely, if only for a little while.

Walking on Brattenvägen, the main thoroughfare between the village and Bratten, he heard the noise of the approaching mopeds from far away. The island was otherwise perfectly silent on this Sunday afternoon, as heavy clouds hung overhead and rain was in the air. Many of the island youths drove motorized vehicles, from small- to medium-sized motorcycles or three-wheeled front-loading mopeds. They spent a lot of time working on and tuning their engines, making them go way faster than allowed and louder than necessary, some with large exhaust pipes in polished chrome sticking out from their vehicles.

Tore chuckled at it all. It was an almost endearing tradition. He'd seen exhaust pipes suitable for a truck on lawnmower-sized engines, but it kept the kids out of trouble, mostly. There were accidents, although they would rarely be reported to the authorities, as all involved parties were well aware of the consequences for their kids and the vehicles involved. Tore shook his head. Just recently, there had been an accident with a golf cart, and neither vehicle had been insured. Hopefully, they'd have learned their lesson.

As he approached the Tudor-style home in the final curve before the straight stretch to Bratten, the mopeds came flying around the corner, approaching him at high speeds. Spotting Tore, the leader of the group slowed down and came to a complete stop.

"Oy, faggot! What are you doing out here on the streets? Shouldn't you be looking for your faggot lover, huh?" The boy was laughing at his own witty words.

Tore froze in place. Was this child talking to him? He hadn't heard the F-word in decades and was so surprised he couldn't respond. He simply stared at the youth, who took it as a sign to continue.

"You deaf or what? What are you staring at me for? Are you attracted to me? Eww, that's gross." He revved the moped and looked at his pals, who were snickering behind him. "Let's get out of here before he gives us AIDS or monkeypox!" Grinning broadly, he shook his head and pulled down the vizor of his helmet, but before he drove off, he pointed at Tore. "You watch out, faggot! We know where you live." Then he laughed, let the gear kick in, and drove off with his friends, leaving Tore standing there like a wet dog in the pouring rain.

It took him a while to will his feet to move again, and when he did, he turned around and headed for home. He no longer felt the desire to go out and be with people. Shaken to the core, barely able to walk, a dreadful thought began to form in the back of his mind. What if Lennart's accident had not been an accident after all? What if it had been a crime—a hate crime even? Tore decided to call the police and talk to the two officers in charge of the Missing Persons Unit. Maybe they could bring in those kids and talk to them.

– 14 –

September 20, 2022

"COME ON, KARL-ERIK. You were the one who wanted me to get fresh air."

Märta pushed her walker in front of her, annoyed that her husband had stopped yet again for some reason. She loved him, sure, but why couldn't he just walk beside her until they reached their destination? They were en route to her secret spot to pick mushrooms, mostly chanterelles. Having just returned from a long stint at Sahlgrenska University Hospital after a stroke, Märta was happy to be home again on her beloved Styrsö, the island where she had been born and, if she had any say in the matter, would die in her own bed. The prospect of dying in a hospital or, worse, a lonely room in Styrsö's nursing home terrified her. To lose your independence like that, having to rely on others to wake you, dress you, feed you? Unbearable. Unthinkable.

The stroke had come out of the blue, but she'd been lucky. The ambulance and the helicopter arrived quickly, and she was flown straight to the hospital. What a commotion, yet she felt privileged to have been treated so promptly and so well. She may not have survived otherwise. She still felt the aftereffects, hence the stupid walker. She'd never needed any help in the past, but these days, it was safer. It didn't keep her from going out into the forest, but she couldn't leave the path and get to her favorite spots. Today would be a test.

Karl-Erik had acquiesced, at last, and agreed to accompany her. Yet every time he joined her for a walk, he invariably fell behind. He was a few years older and didn't walk very well. She knew that, yet here she was, with a walker, always ten steps ahead of him.

"Come on, Karl-Erik! It's just a few more steps and we'll be there," she encouraged while her husband huffed and puffed loudly behind her, looking miserable. Märta pressed on, pushing her walker along the uneven path. She was exhausted, tired from the walk, tired from having to use this god-awful contraption, yet being out in the open air, having all those stately trees around her with the promise of picking enough mushrooms for a delightful dinner was enough of a driving force for her to keep going.

Coming around the corner, she knew she was close. There was her secret spot, the one all her friends wanted her to share with them, but she never had. Of course, anyone could stumble upon it and make it theirs, too, but for as long as she was able to come here, this was hers, and only hers.

Waiting for Karl-Erik to catch up, she stopped and looked around, taking in the landscape. There was something ethereally soothing about the forest, the gentle rustling of the leaves in the wind, oak, birch, and elm. Then there were all the pines and spruces that had been planted in the late nineteenth and early twentieth centuries by school children on the island at the behest of visitors from the East Coast, where they had always been prevalent. Here, the oak had traditionally played first fiddle, but every single oak had been cut down to build ships, as it provided the best timber. Märta wondered what the islands had looked like in the Middle Ages, before the oak had been decimated. That must've been quite the sight! She'd only seen the pictures from Styrsö at the turn of the previous century, after the oaks were gone, the island left barren with not a shrub in sight. Still, spruce and pine were good for mushrooms, so she couldn't complain. Plus she loved the smell of those trees. Bliss.

She spotted a large windthrow she couldn't recall seeing before. "Karl-Erik, I don't remember that one. Is it new?"

He didn't respond—he had no eye for these things—so Märta went on.

"I remember Papa telling us about them, warning us of the dangers of windthrows. There was this kid Pappa was playing with who was crushed by one when it sprang back into place. He died after having his legs and hip broken. It took ten large men to dig him out from underneath, but it was too late." Her face twitched as she imagined the scene. The young boy had been a friend of her father's, and having to witness that must have been traumatic. Even though it was more than sixty years ago that her father had told her the story, it remained with her for her entire life, and she'd made sure to pass it on to her daughters.

"This is odd. Come here, Karl-Erik!" She pointed at another windthrow. "That one is definitely new. You can tell from the tree that it was in the ground not that long ago. The needles are still green. But I distinctly remember another one over there, about fifty meters from here. It was one of the waypoints I use, and it's gone. I can't see it anymore."

Her husband arrived and stood next to her, panting. He looked into the forest and frowned. "I don't know what you're talking about. There are so many windthrows on this island, how can you be sure which ones are new or if one has gone? That makes absolutely no sense."

"I have a nose for these things. Trust me. Now please, help me. I need to check it out. See if there are any mushrooms over there." Märta put the walker in parking mode and stretched out her hand toward her husband, who took it.

"Are you sure that's wise?" He looked worried but led her off the trail and onto the uneven forest floor anyway.

"I need to check out that windthrow. What if someone got stuck underneath it, you know, like little Erik?" She'd told the story so many times, she assumed he would remember it. He did not.

"Erik who?"

"Don't you remember? Pappa's friend. I was just talking about him. He was crushed by a windthrow and didn't survive."

"Oh, *that* Erik! But that was ages ago. Why would anyone get crushed under a windthrow today? When did you last see a child play in the forest, dear? Kids today are more likely to be crushed by their smart devices."

"Come on, help me. We need to go this way." Undeterred, Märta led her husband through the trees. "I am one hundred percent sure that something has changed here. This is not what it looked like the last time I was here."

"Mother," as Karl-Erik lovingly referred to his wife, "you were hospitalized for two weeks and then spent two months in short-term rehab. You have to at least acknowledge the possibility that some things are not how you remember them. The windthrow you miss is probably the one over there. You're just confused."

Märta gave her husband a look that told him what she thought of that statement. "I've spent my entire life on this island. I know every rock and every tree by heart. If I tell you there was a large windthrow over there, then there was one. Let's go check it out."

After a few minutes of walking at a seventy-degree angle away from the path, they got to the place where Märta thought there had been a windthrow.

"See," Karl-Erik said triumphantly. "There's nothing here but a tree stub."

Märta's forehead creased as she stared at the short stump. It looked strange. First of all, it hadn't been cut, nor had it broken off the way a tree would in the wind, where the trunk would crack about three or four feet up; this one had broken off very low down. Secondly, the massive root system that had previously been exposed to the elements was now back in its hole in the ground.

Supported by her husband, she kneeled to inspect it more closely. "This is odd. I swear, this wasn't like this last fall when I was up here. This tree has snapped back into place."

"That's preposterous. How is that possible? I can see how it might happen if the trunk was still intact and the weight had suddenly shifted. But this? Look at it. It's so old and rotten."

"I don't know. But look over there, where the mushrooms are. This is my spot. I know it. And right here, this was the windthrow. It's snapped back, I'm telling you."

"That makes no sense unless someone put it back on purpose. Or maybe this happened a long time ago and you just don't remember it properly?" Karl-Erik tried again. She could see from his face he still thought her memory was playing tricks on her.

"What if it *was* put back on purpose?" she said. "Ever since you told me about poor Lennart, I've been wondering where he disappeared to. What if he came here to look for mushrooms and the windthrow fell on him?

"Are you out of your mind? Why would he be under a windthrow in the middle of the forest? The police called off the search because they think he more than likely fell into the water and drowned."

"I know what the police say. But he was a Pathfinder, and we all know how they love to spend time in the forest."

"You mean he came here for your mushrooms and was crushed? Don't you think there would be signs? He was a tall man."

Märta shrugged. "Yes, but what if it wasn't an accident? What if he was killed and hidden here?"

Karl-Erik laughed at the suggestion. "Don't you think you're being a bit dramatic? The chances of Lennart's disappearance being a natural occurrence are infinitely greater than your cockamamy stories! Why would anyone kill him? That's just preposterous." Karl-Erik wasn't buying it at all, but then, his memory wasn't the most reliable either.

"I don't know. It's not like we were close friends. We went to school together, but that was a long time ago. I don't know what kind of life he led, what might cause anyone to do this to him."

"You're jumping to conclusions. You see a windthrow and see murder. That is a big step…"

Still, Märta felt strongly that something was amiss here. Suddenly, she no longer thought of the mushrooms growing all around her. She needed to get back home and alert Tore. He could inform the police. A cold shiver ran down her back, making her even more certain that she was on to something. What if Lennart was hidden underneath the tree? The poor man. She owed him this much.

– 15 –

September 20, 2022

A T FIRST, THE police were not convinced. "Listen, Tore," Peter, the police inspector began, "I understand that you find it difficult to accept your husband drowned, but accidents like that do happen. We have dozens of accidental drownings in Sweden every year."

"That's not the point. I know Märta. If she says the place looks as if someone purposely did something to it, I believe her. I grew up around here. Märta's little brother was my best friend in school. I know how much she loves to rummage for mushrooms in the forest. She knows the interior of the island like the back of her hand. If she says that the windthrow has snapped back into place, I take her at her word. All I ask is that you look into it. Don't you have equipment for that sort of search?"

"We do. We'd need a cadaver dog. They're specifically trained to find corpses. Sadly, at this point, we don't have specialized dogs anymore. But I'm sure one of our regular dogs would be able to find a body. If push comes to shove, we could always try to lift the windthrow, but as I said, I'm not convinced. We've spoken to so many of your friends and neighbors, and nobody, and I mean that, Tore, nobody had a motive to kill and hide Lennart.

"From what I gather, both you and Lennart are well-liked by your neighbors, and nobody knew of anyone who may have wanted to hurt him. Sure, there is lingering homophobia, especially among some of your religious neighbors and the hormonal teens out there, but even they respect your work for the community. They may not approve of you, but to go from disapproval to killing someone is an enormous step.

"We've followed up on every lead you've sent us, but so far, we've drawn blank after blank. There just isn't anyone with a motive to kill Lennart. Trust me, this was an accident, and in time, his body will wash ashore somewhere. I hate to say this, but in my entire professional career, I've never seen anyone kill a neighbor just like that, not to mention going through the trouble of burying someone in the middle of the forest under a windthrow." He paused for a second as if to consider the suggestion. "Although I have to say, it would make a pretty good hiding spot…"

Tore could almost hear the police inspector thinking.

"Okay, here's what I'll do. I'll organize a dog handler to go search the spot where your friend said she thinks something was out of order. But once that's done and they don't find anything, you will promise to stop calling me, okay? This investigation is officially closed and ruled as an accidental drowning. If Lennart's body ever washes ashore, an autopsy will automatically be performed to rule out any foul play. We've informed neighboring countries where we can reasonably assume that ocean currents could wash the body ashore to keep their eyes open. That's what I can offer you. Is that acceptable to you?"

Tore's chest swelled with hope. "Yes, Peter, of course. But I'm telling you. You'll find him there! I'd go dig myself, but I can't lift those roots."

"Yeah, don't do anything stupid, you hear me? Ideally, make sure Märta and anyone else stays away until we've had a chance to do a proper investigation. Just in case. I'd hate to have a contaminated scene to deal with."

***

Two days later, the police informed Tore that they were on their way to the island with a dog team. They had interviewed Märta and her husband by phone, and she had volunteered to take them to the spot in the forest where she had found the suspicious overturned windthrow. Tore wanted to tag along, but the police thought it better if he did not.

Not that they believed they would find anything, but better to be safe than sorry. They wouldn't allow Märta anywhere close by either. She simply had to point out the spot and let the police dog and their handler do the rest. The dog, however, didn't find any human traces, and the search was called off again. There was nothing unnatural about the site. It was just a windthrow that had snapped back into place. Why, nobody knew.

The police called Tore to let him know they had found nothing and reiterated what they'd said all along: the most likely scenario was that Lennart had drowned.

– 16 –

September 25, 2022

"TORE, WAIT UP! I need to talk to you."

"Bert, what is it now?" He stopped in his tracks, but he didn't want to talk to him, not again. Bert was one of the wealthier men on the island but not very well-liked. He'd moved to Styrsö in the early seventies and had met the daughter of one of the old island families. Having made a fortune in real estate, Bert was very influential and by now owned half the island, or so it seemed. He sported a thin mustache on his upper lip, and what little hair he had left was combed over his bald scalp. It was ridiculous to see him pull a comb from his pants pocket every few minutes and given the windy conditions on the island truly a regular necessity. People jokingly referred to him as "Camembert," a play on the words for "comb" and "Bert" in Swedish. The fact that he often appeared unkempt and smelly didn't help. *Strange for a man so wealthy.*

"I just wanted to catch up and ask you about the topic we discussed a couple of days ago."

"If you're wondering if I've changed my mind, I haven't— and I won't. Not as long as I'm alive."

"Is this about Lennart? I'm very sorry for your loss, and I know, of course, that he owned the property. Your family never had much money." Bert made a dismissive gesture. "Look, this is business. As I've already told you, your plot is the last one I need to complete the set. And to show my appreciation for the unique situation you're in, I'm willing to sweeten my offer. Name your price."

Tore looked at the man who'd caught up to him and was now standing in front of him, blocking his way through the forest. "What do you mean, name your price?"

"I mean exactly what I said. Give me a number. How much would it take for you to sell me that plot now that it's yours?" Bert smiled broadly and pulled out his comb, raking it over his scalp. Tore shook his head, amused despite the situation.

"Look, Bert, I don't think you understand. I have no reason to sell to you. Why does it have to be Lennart's land? You already own half the property on the island. Why is this particular plot so important? It's not as if you can build on it."

"I'm more than willing to trade that plot with another property I own. Or I'll pay handsomely for it."

"It's not about money, and it's not about land. I don't want to build, and Anna isn't going to come back here anyway. But this particular plot is very important to me for very personal reasons. In time, you can buy the other properties Lennart owned if you want to, but not this one."

"I don't understand. Why? You could live comfortably and even make Anna a very wealthy woman."

Lennart put his hand on Bert's shoulder. "Bert, not everything in the world is about money. I know that's difficult for you to grasp, but for me, some things are more important, even more so now that Lennart is gone. That plot...where it sits is special. I feel connected to him in a way you wouldn't understand. Beyond that, it's none of your business. Once I'm dead, you can pester Anna about it."

"Is there nothing I can do to convince you?" Bert asked one last time.

Refusing to engage with Bert any further, Tore walked past him and continued on his way through the forest. He was upset. Why would Bert not give up? What was he up to? It was very suspicious. When he was back home, he'd call the police to let them know about it.

***

Peter, the police inspector, sighed. "Tore, please, you need to let it go. This is no longer on my table. It's with the Missing Persons Unit. Talk to them."

"But you're the one I know…" the old man tried.

Peter chuckled on the other end of the line. "All right, Tore. Here's what I'll do. I'll have someone look into this, but don't expect anything. True, it is suspicious that Bert's prepared to pay so much more than the plot is worth, but it makes no sense that someone would kill Lennart over a piece of property while his husband is still alive."

"Unless Bert thought Anna or I would be more willing to sell it than Lennart was?"

"May I ask why it's so special to you—and Bert, for that matter? Why won't you sell?"

"It's a long story. When Lennart and I first met, we didn't have anywhere to go, to be alone. We couldn't go to my house, as it was too small and we had no privacy, plus I wasn't out at the time. Lennart was, but his parents didn't approve of him being gay, so going to his house was out of the question, too. We had to meet outdoors, at a place in the forest. It's not too far from Stora Rös, with beautiful views out west but still protected by surrounding trees. There we could meet in private and be alone to talk. At the time, I didn't even know it was family property. I only learned about that after Lennart's parents passed."

"I see. That makes sense. And because of that, you don't want to sell?"

"I don't want to defile the place by selling it. Anna doesn't know, we've never told her, and I'd appreciate it if you didn't tell her either. Once I'm dead it won't matter. I want Anna to do what she thinks is best for her regardless of what Lennart or I felt. Besides, once we're gone, the place loses its significance. But I just couldn't…"

"Don't worry, Tore. This isn't going to end up in any notes, and I won't mention it to Anna. Thank you for telling me, though. Your secret is safe with me. I completely understand why you would want to hold on to this plot. The value it holds for you, given what you had to go through when you were younger, cannot be measured in money. I'll keep you posted if we find anything, okay?"

September 27, 2022

"Fuck, it's cold today!" Bosse blew into his hands and rubbed them together again. "We'd better find those lobster pots well filled."

Roger laughed and shook his head. He and his best friend had been fishing for lobster for many years, and Bosse complained about the cold every time. What did he expect in late September on the Swedish West Coast? Of course, the mornings were always the coldest. They'd taken advantage of the sunny weather yesterday to place their pots in their usual places. They weren't alone. This spot just west of Styrsö was popular with a lot of locals. The black gold of the sea, as lobsters were called in Swedish, preferred to hang around rocks and boulders on the ground at a depth of thirty to ninety feet, and there weren't many areas where the Kattegat got this deep near the islands. Every family had a favorite spot to drop their pots, hoping to catch the coveted crustaceans. At the first auction of the season, a kilo of lobster could sell for as much as a hundred thousand Swedish kronor—almost ten thousand US dollars.

Bosse and Roger had both been raised on the island, and both could trace their family roots hundreds of years back, all islanders; fishermen, farmers, and sailors, proud residents of a world that for centuries was very different from the mainland and also rather isolated from it. It wasn't until after the end of the Cold War in 1997 that the islands were even made accessible to tourists without prior approval from the military and secret police.

By that point, Bosse and Roger had already been fishing lobster for years, as well as mackerel, cod, and other delicacies from the cool waters of the Kattegat. Come late September, locals, visitors, and summer guests alike would take to their boats, some bigger, most smaller, and drive out along the coast, marine maps in hand, to find what they each deemed the best spot to drop their pots in the water, armed with slightly rotten fish to attract the lobsters from their hiding spots in their preferred stony hunting grounds.

Bosse and Roger had found an excellent spot that they returned to every year. Bosse, cold as his hands were this beautiful morning, steered their console boat out from the marina at Styrsö Tången and due southwest through the channel between Styrsö and Vargö, past the Sandvik harbor and straight toward the small islet of Hästbåden. Here, there were several large areas with rocks protruding from the seabed, some taller than others, but all potential homes and hunting grounds for lobster. Having set out their twelve pots the day before, Bosse and Roger would return more or less every morning until the end of November. They had to get out early, as they both had jobs in the city. Once they'd checked the pots, emptied them of lobsters, crabs, and the odd fish that might've gotten caught, they'd stock them again and put them back into the water for another day.

Any catch would be stored in a creel, tagged with their name, in case the police or coast guard came by to investigate. They knew better than to cheat, but not everybody cared about all the laws and regulations of the country. They did and always had, as they'd been properly raised by their fathers. This year, the government had decided that the minimum size of a lobster to keep was nine centimeters across the shield, measured from the eye socket to the back of the main shield. Smaller animals had to be released back into the sea to grow some more.

After a fifteen-minute ride, they arrived at their first buoy. It was a round, white one with the letter F in black taped to it. The F indicated that they were not professionals. Each fisherman had their own buoy to distinguish it from others, properly marking them with a name and a phone number.

Bosse slowed the boat as they approached, and Roger got on his knees in the bow so he could reach the buoy and pull up the lobster pot attached to it with a line. He pulled and pulled, and the grin on his face indicated that they'd gotten something. "It's heavy!" After a minute, the pot breached the surface, and Roger pulled it aboard.

"Seems we got lucky! There's two in here, one is a big one." There was pride in his voice. "Congratulations! The first two lobsters of the 2022 season are aboard." He reached into his jacket to pull out the measuring tool and then opened the pot and grabbed one of the two lobsters from behind and pulled it out. He measured it even though he knew it was bigger than it had to be. "This one is a whooping twelve centimeters. What a beauty!" He dropped it into the creel and picked up the second one. "This one's smaller." Roger measured it and let out a sigh "Nah, it's only eight and a half." He gently dropped it back into the water, and the lobster quickly disappeared into the dark. "Oh well, we've got eleven more pots to check."

They drove a few meters to a different spot. Here, another stone formation protruded from the seabed, and as no other pots were nearby, they dropped their now-empty pot in. After that, they proceeded to the next one to check it out, and the next. This went on for quite some time, as each buoy had to be identified first, the pot pulled up, checked, potentially emptied, lobsters measured, the pot restocked with bait, and lowered again.

Roger's arm was starting to ache, and they switched positions, with Bosse taking charge of the pot checking. "The next one is going to be full! I have a good feeling about it. We always catch big ones in this area." he shouted back at Roger, who was carefully navigating their small craft between all the buoys placed in the area and other boats out there with them, checking their pots. "Over there. I think that's ours!" Bosse pointed to the starboard.

"I see it." Roger nodded, turned the boat, and steered it slowly toward the white buoy in the water in front of them.

"Got it," Bosse said and checked the name tag just to be sure. Then he began to pull it up, but after a few tugs concluded it was stuck, which was not unheard of. He pulled a bit more, to no avail. "This thing seems stuck. I can't get it off the ground. It's moving a little, can you see? But it's not coming loose."

"Maybe it got stuck to an anchor or some other trash on the seabed. Let me change position and you can try again. The line is strong and won't break easily. Hang on!"

Roger moved the boat around to a slightly different angle to the pot and stopped again. Bosse tried again, pulling and yanking. After a few more attempts of this and another change in position, he finally felt movement. While a lobster pot was a fairly lightweight construction, once submerged and possibly filled with crustaceans, it did feel much heavier to pull up, and Bosse began to pant after a short while. "This one's heavy, just as I thought."

Roger laughed. "Either that or you're out of shape, buddy."

"Very funny." Bosse noticed the pot was breaching the surface. "Here we go." He quickly grabbed it with one hand and with the other lifted it out of the water and into the boat. "Wow, this one is crawling with lobsters. There are at least four in here. That's unusual."

He opened the side door and grabbed the first one and measured it. "Ten centimeters! Perfect." He dropped it into the creel and grabbed the next one. "Eleven." A broad grin spread across his face as he showed Roger the lobster before dropping it into the creel. "Looks like we'll have one for every family member tonight."

As he pulled out the last lobster, he noticed something else inside the pot, probably a small dead fish, although that seemed odd. He measured the lobster and released it back into the water as it wasn't big enough before turning his attention to the dead fish. It was stuck in the thread of the pot, and he had to untangle it, which was when he noticed that it wasn't a fish but a finger. Instinctively, he let out a scream and dropped it.

"What's the matter?" Roger asked, looking puzzled from behind the boat's steering wheel.

"That was no dead fish. It was a finger."

"A finger? Do you mean a human finger?"

"Duh! I doubt we'd catch fish fingers here, don't you? Oh my God! We need to alert the authorities. Log the position we're at. I'm sure the police will want to send in divers."

Roger waymarked their position in the boat's GPS and picked up his cell phone, dialing 1-1-2.

"SOS Alarm? Good morning. This is Roger Nyström. We're out here in the southern archipelago near Hästbåden, fishing for lobster, and we just picked up a human finger in one of our pots. Can you patch me through to the police?" Waiting for the call to be transferred, Roger watched as Bosse threw all the lobsters back into the water. He couldn't blame him. His appetite for a lobster dinner had vanished as well. Given what these critters likely had been eating for supper recently, who was to say that they, by extension, couldn't be considered cannibals? The thought had his stomach give up its contents just as the police responded.

"Hello? I'm sorry." He retched over the side of the boat. "I had a bit of an incident with my stomach," he explained, looking over at his old friend, who was ghostly pale, as the realization slowly sank in. "I think we found a dead body. You need to come out here to dive for it. We just dragged up a finger in one of our lobster pots."

Roger listened as the police officer on the other side asked a question.

"How do I know it's a finger? Seriously? It has two joints and a fingernail, and from the looks of it, it's been in the water for a while." Describing the finger to the police had his stomach churning again. "Please, can we just drop it off with you guys and you can take it from there? I don't want this thing in my boat any longer than necessary."

Roger listened to the instructions from the police officer.

"The sea police? Yeah, sure. We can wait. Half an hour? Are you kidding me? Well, tell them to hurry up." He hung up.

"What did they say?" Bosse's face was ashen, and his voice lacked all luster.

"The sea police are coming to pick up the finger from us. They want us to wait here. Fuck, it's cold. Did we bring any coffee?"

The mere mention of the brew had Bosse throw up again, and Roger could've hit himself. Stupid idea!

"Sorry, pal! I don't think I could drink anything either."

After Bosse had calmed himself and his stomach had stopped releasing any content potentially left inside, he moved to the back of the boat and sat next to Roger. "Do we have anything to wrap that thing up? I know this sounds awful, but it seems almost as if it's staring at me."

"You can't even see it from here," Roger replied, fishing for tissues in his jacket. "Here! This might do." He tried to hand them to Bosse, who shook his head.

"I'm not touching that again!"

Roger laughed. He wasn't going to touch it either. They kept the boat more or less stationary. Dropping anchor was completely out of the question given what they might drag up from below.

They fell silent for a while, each man staring out into the distance and the darkness whose veil was slowly lifting from the east. The lighthouse of Vinga was still flashing, once every thirty seconds, a comforting beacon to their troubled minds.

Absently, Bosse wondered, "Who do you think it is?"

Roger shrugged. "I don't know. I doubt the police will ever tell us unless, of course, it's someone we know."

Before he could say anything else, a small dinghy approached and drew up alongside their boat. "Morning, guys. No luck?" It was Anton, another local guy from Styrsö.

Bosse didn't know how to respond, but Roger dismissed him with a laugh. "Quite the contrary. You'll likely read about it in the papers…" He stretched out his arms as wide as he could.

"Good for you guys. I've got one more to check. It's been a great day so far. I'll leave you to it. Have a good one!" Anton raised his arm in farewell and sped up his boat.

There were a handful of other boats in the area, but right now, no one was approaching them, and based on the lack of buoys in the water around them, no one would need to unless it was a friend who wanted to catch up or brag. But like them, most would only go out, check their pots, and then go to work.

Suddenly, a thought struck Bosse. "What about Lennart? They haven't found his body yet, and the police said he likely drowned."

"Possible! Did you recognize the finger?" Roger teased.

"I told you, I'm not going near that thing." Bosse shuddered at the thought of having to look at the finger again, never mind touch it. It had been so disgusting.

"We'll just have to leave it to the police. I'm sure they can do a DNA analysis or something. And if they find the rest of the body, it'll bring closure to whoever. To be honest, I don't think it's Lennart. You think he'd be dragged all the way out here by ocean currents?"

Even as he said it, Roger wasn't convinced. They could see Salskärs Udde from their boat. It was only a couple of miles to the northeast, and with ocean currents, one never knew. *Poor sod.* He knew the old man, of course, like one knew everybody on the island, even though Lennart was much older. Given his relationship with Tore, the two were local celebrities of sorts, and everybody on the island had an opinion about them, especially all those years ago, when they first became a couple.

Incredibly brave, Lennart and Tore had stayed. They had endured the bullying, the name-calling, and the endless visits by pastors and know-it-alls who had offered to pray on their behalf. Roger had been privy to countless Sunday-afternoon discussions around his grandparents' kitchen table, where they would always have dinner after service, to hear the latest gossip his mother and his grandmother had picked up in the pews and at church coffee afterward.

As lost as both men were in their reveries, the siren from the police boat alerted them to the approaching vessel.

− 18 −

October 11, 2022

Anna Svensson?"

Anna didn't recognize the voice nor the government 010-number from where the call came. "Yes, this is she."

"This is Peter Gustavson, Gothenburg police."

"Peter. What can I do for you?"

"I have news. And it is important."

"Oh?" She wasn't sure what to make of that. First of all, she hadn't heard from the police in weeks, and with her pa still missing and likely drowned, what they were all waiting for was just the official pronunciation of death, which she'd learned would take years. So what did he want?

"We may have a lead in finding your father." The statement was matter of fact, but to Anna, it was earth-shattering.

"Is he a-alive?"

"No. I'm afraid not. A couple of fishermen found a finger in a lobster pot a couple of weeks ago. I just received the DNA results and need to make sure it matches a relative's DNA. You are his biological daughter, aren't you? Would you please come to Gothenburg so we can do a test on you?"

A finger? That's all that was left of Pa? Anna wailed and screamed into the phone. While she had accepted that her father was dead a long time ago, the absurdity of this call was overwhelming. Not only did it reopen a barely cauterized wound but it also drove a stick into her heart, twisting and turning it for good measure. Ali, who was still in the bathroom, came running out.

"Habeebti? What happened?" He took her into his arms and picked up the phone she'd dropped on the floor.

"Hello?" he said into the device.

"Yes, hello? This is Peter Gustavsson from the police in Gothenburg. Is Anna all right?"

"No, she's not. What did you tell her?"

"We found a body part, but we need to do a DNA comparison to make sure it's Anna's father. We have no other missing people in the area. Therefore, there's a strong likelihood this is Lennart Svensson. I'm sorry I can't bring better news. Do you think I can speak to her?"

Crouching on the floor, phone in one hand, his arm around a heap of flesh, Ali tried to get the police officer on speaker. "Habeebti? Please can you talk to him?"

Sniveling, Anna nodded. Ali extricated himself and pushed the speaker button on Anna's phone. Sitting on the floor together, Ali put his arm around his partner again. "Okay, Peter, we're listening. You're on speakers."

"Thank you. Ali, I presume?"

"Yes, it is." He'd met the police officer back on Styrsö during the extensive search for his now likely dead almost father-in-law. He had an excellent memory. Probably part of the job description as a good police officer.

"Please allow me to apologize for not bringing better news. Do you think you can come to Gothenburg any time soon?"

Weakly, Anna responded, "Are you going to dive at the spot where you found the finger to see if the rest of the body is down there?"

"Not right away, no. The weather in the coming days is not suitable. Let us first find out whose finger it was. Once we know more, we'll decide on the next steps. I've been told by my colleagues at the sea police that the area where the finger was found is subject to currents. The finger may have been severed for some reason and the body could have been transported elsewhere. For all we know, it could wash ashore in Denmark or somewhere farther along the Swedish coast at some point. Or it belongs to someone who drowned elsewhere. It's difficult to predict how drowned bodies will behave. I'd rather not go into detail, but once we have an identity, we'll decide on the next steps. Okay?"

"Thanks, I appreciate that. I'm not sure this is an image I need in my head. So if the DNA from the finger matches my father, then what?"

"Well, at that point, you get closure, albeit not the kind you may have hoped for. It will be a confirmation that your father drowned. He'll be pronounced dead, and you can move on with your life."

"I see." Anna's voice was weak but steady. "Have you told my dad yet?"

"No, I have not. I was hoping you might break the news to him in person. I think he may need to have you by his side when he finds out. A few hours more or less won't make a difference, will they?"

"Agreed. We'll fly down as soon as we can. Thank you for letting us know. Is there anything else you need to tell us?"

"Not at this stage. Call me once you've arrived in town. Thank you." The line disconnected.

Still sitting on the floor, Ali rocked Anna to console her. He knew, of course, that nothing would. He'd seen it in Aleppo, friends and family members disappearing. Some were never found again, and others popped up out of the blue, dumped in alleys or, worse, morgues, their bodies bruised and battered. No one was ever held accountable, regardless of how obvious the torture wounds were. Families were content to get their loved ones back, to be able to nurse them back to health or to bury them, to get some semblance of closure.

Ali was confident that here, in Sweden, the police would do their utmost to get answers for Anna and her father, to find out what had happened to Lennart. Whether or not they'd succeed was another thing entirely. But they would try. That counted for something.

After sitting on the floor for some time, Anna calmed down and complained that her legs had fallen asleep. "I need to get to Dad."

– 19 –

October 12, 2022

SITTING NEXT TO each other on the plane to Gothenburg, Ali was stuck in the middle seat while Anna sat by the window, looking out without seeing, her head resting against the cool, hard fuselage. Ali held her hand, trying to console her, as if this tactile motion of his thumb across the back of her hand might induce some additional strength, a strength she'd need to face her father soon.

They sat mostly in silence, and the atmosphere around them was laden. The businessman sitting next to Ali in the aisle seat paid them no attention, not that it mattered when they were in a world of their own. After touching down at Landvetter Airport, they exited the plane and swiftly made their way to the taxi queue. Ali instructed the driver from the back seat to take them straight to Saltholmen and to hurry up. They had forty-five minutes until the next ferry left for the islands. The driver looked at Ali as if to say *who are you to talk to me in this way?* but seeing Anna's ashen face, he turned back, never saying what had been on his mind. In fact, he drove them to the harbor without saying a single word, making sure they made the ferry in good time.

They reached the island half an hour later and walked the distance from Tången to the house. Anna was nervous, afraid of how Tore would react. Simply showing up at the house would be bad enough. The second he opened the door, he'd know that something was amiss. Should she knock? Or just walk in like she always had? No, she couldn't just walk in. Given what he'd been through, that could scare him, and she couldn't do that to him.

So they knocked, which felt insanely weird. This was her home, after all. *Home.*

There was no reaction for some time, but Anna knew her dad was home. The lights were on. So they waited. After a few minutes, they heard the shuffle of approaching feet inside. Tore opened the door, and when he saw Anna and Ali, he froze. After what amounted to a few seconds but felt a lot longer, Anna noticed the tears appearing in his eyes as he formulated the words she knew he'd say.

"Have they found him?"

She began to cry anew and crossed the distance to him and hugged him. "Maybe, Dad. Maybe they have. Let's go inside."

Once they were sitting at the kitchen table, Anna took Tore's hand and looked him in the eyes. "Dad, I know this is not what you wanted to hear, but the police have found a finger. They need my DNA to confirm it's Pa."

Tore stared straight ahead, his eyes not focused on anything in particular. "A finger? What about the rest of the body?"

Anna shook her head. "I don't know. I presume the police won't just send a dive team on a whim. They probably want to make sure the finger is Pa's before they go look for the rest, and the weather is really bad right now, with the strong western winds. I don't know."

"Okay. Well, if we get confirmation that this is Lennart, then it's best to assume he got a sea burial and leave it at that. Maybe it might be better if they'd let him rest down there in peace." Tore was astonishingly stoic under the circumstances. "But there's something we need to discuss before you go to the police for the DNA test. Something you need to know...and I don't want you to find out from a swab test." Tore lowered his gaze and avoided Anna's eyes as if he were ashamed.

Anna felt the impending bad news almost physically constrict her airways. What would a DNA test possibly reveal other than identifying that the finger had been Pa's? Did he—and she, too— have some sort of hereditary condition? But then, that wouldn't be revealed by a police DNA test.

"What do you mean, Dad?"

Tore took a deep breath. "There's no easy way to say this, not after all these years. But since you're about to find out anyway, let me be the one to break it to you. Pa was not your father—not biologically, anyway."

– 20 –

October 12, 2022

"WHAT ARE YOU talking about?" Anna demanded, upset. "He's listed as the father on my birth certificate along with my mother. Every extract from the population registry says the same. You're both my fathers, him through birth, you through adoption. You can't forge documents like that."

Tore shifted uncomfortably in his armchair. "Please, let me tell you the story, okay? Afterward, you can judge us." He lifted his head and looked straight at her. Anna said nothing. "Lennart was your uncle, not your father. Your real mother was Lennart's younger sister, Lena. He and I had already begun dating when she became pregnant by a stranger. Seems a recurring theme in that family, I might add. When Lena's parents found out, they sent her to Denmark to have the child and give it up for adoption because they were afraid of the scandal it would cause here on the island. You have to remember that your grandparents were very religious, and premarital sex and abortions were absolutely unacceptable, and still are in some quarters. So, they sent her off before she started showing and concocted some story about a disease that needed treatment abroad.

"When it was time for Lena to give birth to you, Lennart joined her, at his parents' behest, to be with her and make sure she gave up the baby for adoption. But Lena didn't want to give up her child, and Lennart had always wanted to become a father but knew he couldn't. So they cooked up this story together, swatting two flies in one go. They organized a fake ID for her and pretended to be a young Swedish-Danish couple in love.

"Of course, this was before DNA tests were available, and nobody questioned their identities or considered that a couple would fake parenthood. They checked her into the hospital under the fake ID and told the doctors they'd been on vacation when the water broke. Lennart assumed fatherhood, and when he brought you home, the Swedish tax authorities accepted the Danish birth certificate and registered you as his daughter."

Anna felt the floor fall away from underneath her, and had it not been for Ali holding her hand, she might have fallen off the chair. Aunt Lena was her mother? Her fathers had rarely talked about her.

"What happened to Lena?" she asked.

"That's another very sad story. Lena decided to stay in Denmark, as she didn't want to return with Lennart and the baby and face her parents' wrath. She made a wise choice because your grandparents were tremendously upset when Lennart came home with you. They didn't approve, at least, not initially. Then, just a few weeks later, Lena committed suicide. She suffered from postpartum depression, accentuated by the shame of the entire process. When she was brought home to be buried here in the cemetery, your grandparents claimed she'd died because she hadn't responded to treatment for the disease she'd left with, to make sure she ended up in hallowed ground."

Ali shook his head. "This is quite the story. Why haven't you told Anna about this before?"

Tore looked at him with the saddest eyes and let out another deep sigh before responding. "Religion and dogma are extremely powerful driving forces, and on a small island like ours, judgment is probably the worst. People here are kind, they're good. But they will also judge you quickly if you're different, or most will. Anna's grandparents were ashamed. They were ashamed of Lennart, their gay son, who not only defied the dogmas of the Church but also lived openly with his lover in the big city. What is it they say? Love the sinner, not the sin?

"They were also ashamed for failing to raise their daughter properly, which in her case meant abstaining from premarital sex. To top it all off, she killed herself, which is also against Scripture.

They felt strongly that they could not have remained on the island without somehow forcing the square peg into its round hole. So, Lennart and I agreed to never mention this to you, Anna. Initially, we were going to tell you once Grandma Astrid and Grandpa Arvid were dead, but by that point, you had become our daughter in the eyes of everybody, and we just couldn't bring ourselves to tell you the truth."

Anna looked at her father in disbelief. "So you kept lying to me, and you would've taken the truth to your grave?"

Tore looked to the floor again and answered meekly. "I'm sorry, Anna. I really am. It was never our intention to hurt you. We did it to protect you, but what difference does it make? It's not like you can reconnect with your mother."

Feeling Ali squeezing her trembling hand, Anna contemplated what she had been told. Her father was her uncle and her mother had killed herself. Her real father was unknown, possibly still alive, and right here on the island. What a clusterfuck! How would she go on from here? Her entire family history was a lie, constructed to uphold a veneer of normalcy, the appearance of conformity. How sick it all was.

"What was my mother like?" she asked after a long period of uncomfortable silence.

"I didn't know her very well. You have to remember that your father was quite a bit older than Lena, who had been an oops baby, and at the time, we didn't have much contact with his family. Lennart and I lived in the city where we could be ourselves, more or less, and he rarely spoke to them. Again, the whole religious thing drove a wedge between them. Lena came to see us at the studio we rented in town once or twice, but she was just a girl. She hadn't turned eighteen when she got pregnant. But she was beautiful and kind and very spirited. I'm not surprised the boys fell for her.

"After you were born and your father brought you home, your grandparents refused all contact, but eventually, curiosity got the better of them, and on a sunny Saturday afternoon, they suddenly arrived on our doorstep in Majorna, to visit their granddaughter. I guess they had somehow come up with a story to convince their friends in the congregation about how you had come to be. In the choice between a child out of wedlock and a gay son, the former was the lesser evil."

Tore smiled as he reminisced. "You won't remember that day, but I'll never forget it. You were dressed in typical late-seventies apparel, hand-me-downs, of course, cute as a button, sleeping after a meal when they showed up. Grandma Astrid fell in love with you the second she held you in her arms, and Grandpa Arvid would barely let us put you back into your crib. He was grinning at you, talking to you, and rocking you in his arms for the longest time. It was such a beautiful scene to behold. Anna, you were the one who repaired your father's relationship with his parents, and somewhere along the line, they began to tolerate my presence, too." He said those last words with a lot of sadness.

"I had no idea Sweden was so conservative!" Ali said to no one in particular.

"Well," Tore shrugged, "there are very conservative and religious pockets here in Sweden, especially along the coastlines in what were once fishing communities. I guess risking your life at sea on a daily basis is a strong catalyst for religious fervor. At the time and through the eighties and well into the nineties, Gothenburg was an extremely homophobic city and a nest for neo-Nazis, too. Seems like ages ago, but things did change eventually.

"Out here on the islands, the population has always been more religious than the mainland. The southernmost islands are still ruled—for lack of a better word—by the Church to this very day, while Styrsö and Brännö slowly changed along with the rest of the city. We still have a couple of congregations, but as a whole, the island is like any suburb on the mainland. Lennart and I were quite the sensation when we moved out here together after we inherited the house, but today, several queer couples live on the island, and at least two of them have children. The world has changed a lot." Tore laughed. "You can even mow the lawn on a Sunday these days. That wasn't permitted when we first moved here."

"Mow the lawn?" Ali didn't understand.

"It's a thing out here. It used to be against Church rules to work on a Sunday—the Lord's day—so mowing your lawn or doing yard work was frowned upon. But this is Sweden, so God stuck up his middle finger at us and let the sun shine only on Sunday—when you couldn't mow the lawn—then made sure it rained nonstop on Saturday and Monday. I'm exaggerating, of course, but that's how it often felt. This all changed quickly in the late nineties when the priest of the state church was caught mowing the lawn on a Sunday afternoon. After that, everybody began to do it." Tore shook his head. "It's hard to fathom this happened only twenty years ago."

Anna had been listening in silence to their exchange, nodding now and then at something she also remembered. Her mother, her *aunt*, was still on her mind.

"Dad, how come I've never seen a picture of Aunt Lena? I barely even knew I had an aunt, that Pa had a sister."

"After her death, your grandparents destroyed all pictures of her. Even though she officially died from that fake disease and received a Christian burial, I guess it was just too painful for them. We never found a single picture of her when we cleared the house after their sudden passing. It was as if she had never existed. I'm sorry, dear. Maybe you could check with the school? I'm sure there must be class pictures still somewhere. I'd be happy to come along if you want."

Anna shook her head. She felt conflicted. She was about to get confirmation that her father, uncle, was dead. She'd just learned that her real mother was her aunt, who was also dead. Should she even mourn an uncle the way she had expected to mourn a father? "I need to go lie down for a while. I'm not feeling well."

Tore got up and walked over to her. As Anna got up, too, he hugged her. "I'm so sorry, dear. I didn't mean to hurt you or deceive you. You have always been our child. I just couldn't put you through the pain of finding out the truth from a police officer. I will call them and explain, okay?"

Anna didn't respond as she withdrew from her father's arms and allowed Ali to take her upstairs to her childhood bedroom to lie down.

– 21 –

October 27, 2022

Anna and Ali had been back in Stockholm for quite some time when Police Inspector Gustavson called to confirm the remains found were those of Lennart Svensson.

Anna sat down and took a deep breath. Coming to terms with it all had been difficult. No. Difficult was an understatement. Her entire life's foundation had been a sham, blown away like the straw house the little pig had built, and she felt as if she'd been devoured alive. Everything she had ever known was a lie. Yes, her fathers had always been honest about her mother committing suicide, but it wasn't because of a "drunk fling" her pa had during a trip to Frederikshavn. The whole story of Dad forgiving him when he'd come home with the little bundle in his arms was an elaborate and frankly, in hindsight, unbelievable fabrication to cover up an even bigger family secret.

Knowing Pa like she had, the truth made much more sense to Anna than the story they'd told her. It was so much more who he was at heart. Pa was never a cheater, even if he had, apparently, been willing to lie to her and sacrifice her truth to allow her grandparents to save face. Oh, how she had loved her grandparents as a little girl...or so she'd been told. She'd been inconsolable when they died in a car crash in 1985, according to her fathers. She'd been too young to know if this was true but had never questioned it until now. A few months later, the three of them had moved from the city back to Styrsö, into their ancestral home.

She had very few actual recollections of her grandparents, her love for them more like a distant memory, the shadow of emotions, than anything tangible. Thinking back to the family photos of Christmases and Midsummers past, with her grandparents smiling, holding her, she had to wonder: was it all fake? Would she be able to honor Pa's memory knowing he had lied to her about everything? Would she ever be able to forgive him?

"Anna, are you listening?"

"Yes, Inspector, I am. Sorry, just a lot on my mind."

"I can imagine. First of all, my sincere condolences on your loss. Given the story Tore told me about Lennart being your biological uncle, I can't even begin to fathom how you must feel to have learned the truth like this. But the DNA test confirms he was your maternal uncle, i.e. your biological mother's brother."

"What's the next step?" Anna asked. She needed to focus on something procedural to keep her mind straight.

"We're going to send out dive teams to the area. We have the GPS coordinates from the fishermen who found the finger and the patrol who went out there to pick it up. I can't guarantee we will find anything, given ocean currents, but if we do, we'll be able to officially rule out any foul play. I'm sure that will give both you and Tore peace of mind that your father, sorry uncle—"

Anna interrupted him. "It's okay, Peter, you can call him my father. It's how I've known him all my life."

"Okay. Father it is. Anyway, we still believe your father fell, hit his head, and drowned. The body moved with the sea currents, and somehow, the finger got stuck in that lobster pot. Where the rest of his body is, we can't know for sure. It could be stuck behind or under a rock or may have drifted on elsewhere, but it's worth the effort."

"Does my dad know?" Despite everything Anna was still worried how this might affect him.

"I haven't told him about the DNA results yet. I figured you may want to do that. I will, of course, if you'd prefer, but I think it may be easier if it comes from you."

"Yes, I agree. I'll figure out travel arrangements now."

After hanging up, Anna sat at the kitchen table and sobbed in mourning as the truth finally took hold of her conscious mind. But what exactly was it that she was mourning? The death of her father? The death of the fantasy that had been her life?

Did she feel differently about Pa knowing he was her uncle? She didn't know, as the one had become inextricably intertwined with the other. Anna Svensson was a lie. She didn't know who she was anymore. What did it mean to be a dead man's niece rather than his daughter? With no close surviving relatives on that side of the family, she was the last of the biological Svenssons. Did that signify anything? Did it matter?

She and Ali had been to Lena's old high school in the city, and they had found class photos from the years Lena had gone to school there, up until she dropped out because of her pregnancy. It had been eerie to look at the young woman in those photos who so closely resembled Pa—and herself. Yes, they all shared the "Svensson nose." People often commented on how alike Lennart and Anna were. But he was a man, and she was a woman.

Seeing the obvious resemblance to her biological mother, her posture, her hair, and the way she looked into the camera, it was like seeing herself in those images even though they were taken before she had been born. She still had no inkling as to who her real father was. She had grown up with two men as fathers, yet none of them had provided any DNA for her genetic makeup. Did that matter? Should she look for a third father? Or just let it go?

Her dad had gone out of his way to try to make it up to her, but it wasn't his fault, was it? The decision to deceive the world had been her grandparents' and Pa's. Would the alternative have been any better? What if Lena had given her up for adoption? She'd have ended up in the Danish foster system, possibly adopted by an unsuspecting Danish family, never knowing about her real family on the other side of the Kattegat.

All these thoughts and questions had taken their mental toll, so much so that Anna had called in sick at work after returning from Gothenburg. How could she focus on how to best communicate the inner values of others to the public if she didn't even know who she was herself? She hadn't given any details, but her doctor had been willing to sign off on her sick leave.

Through it all, Ali never left her side, her steadfast lighthouse in the stormy sea her life had become. She felt safe with him, never once questioning his motives or if he was who he said he was, which was weird given how her own life had been turned upside down. While others around her sometimes doubted his integrity, for their own questionable reasons, Anna never did. She could think of no reason why he would lie about having fled Syria and narrowly escaped to Europe that fateful summer of 2015 when millions of others also fled the war-torn country.

He had moved in with her, his few physical belongings leaving a distinct mark and adding a homely feel to an apartment that had previously felt more like a hotel suite than an actual home. Even though it had only been a month since they first met, to Anna, it felt as if she'd known Ali much longer. *I guess trauma has that effect on people.*

***

"Dad?"

"Yes, dear, it's me. How are you?" Tore had picked up almost straight away, but he sounded tired. His voice seemed to have aged these past weeks, or maybe it was her imagination.

"Do you have a minute?"

"Of course. What is it I can do for you?"

Anna paused for a moment, putting her hand over her phone and looking up at the ceiling as she gathered strength for what she was about to tell her father. She'd wanted to wait until she and Ali could get to the island, but they'd talked about it during her previous visit, when she'd gone to provide the DNA sample, and they'd agreed to share any news instantly. Regardless of the kind of news, she had to keep that promise. She took a deep breath.

"The police have just called, Dad. They've identified the finger. It was Pa's."

The wail that suddenly erupted on the other end of the line drove tears to Anna's eyes as well, and for a while, they both cried, Anna clutching her phone to her ear.

Tore was the first to speak. "What are they going to do next?"

"They're sending out a dive team to see if there's anything else out there. To see if they can retrieve the rest of the body. If they do, they can do an autopsy and physically rule out foul play."

"Good." Tore was anything but convincing.

"At least we have closure now, Dad. He drowned. They found him. And as tragic as it is, he led a full and productive life, right? That must count for something. We can finally have a funeral and take our leave properly."

"You're right. It's just the finality of it all. Any hope I might have had…" He didn't finish and began crying again.

"I know, I know. But isn't certainty better than not knowing? Isn't closure preferable to hope without there being any?" Anna didn't believe her own words. She'd rather have clung to hope herself, as futile as it might have been. "Listen, we're coming down this weekend, okay? Maybe by then, the authorities will have found something. I miss you, Dad."

Tore seemed surprised by her statement, and into the silence, Anna blurted, "I love you!" All she got in response were more tears before the line disconnected. It was a tiny first step toward what Anna hoped would lead to reconciliation. The journey ahead would undoubtedly be long.

She looked at her calendar for the coming days and noticed a dinner invitation from her boss, Anders, for Friday night. She couldn't wiggle herself out of that. It was too important to miss. Besides, they had some big news. Secretly, Anna hoped it might be a promotion after she had pulled off the firm's first political campaign. She texted Ali to see if he was available for a quick trip to Gothenburg over the weekend.

Despite the pain of learning about her mother and the deception, she also felt a renewed sense of loss of her father and a growing need to rebuild her relationship with Dad before it was too late.

Ali was quick to respond, only worrying about the cost of the trip.

Don't worry, honey, Anna texted back. *I'll deal with that. Would you like to take a train for a change?*

– 22 –

October 28, 2022

THE REPERCUSSIONS OF the phone call still weighing on her, Anna and Ali took the bus out to Anders's house in the Stockholm archipelago. Unlike its counterpart on the West Coast, the islands here were mostly connected by bridges, and there was car traffic almost everywhere, except on the outermost band of islands.

She had not returned to work all week, but this was more of a private function, and Anders, her boss, had insisted—gently—that she come. As they walked up to the house, she contemplated how much her life had changed in recent weeks. It felt almost like a dream as she emerged from the elevator with her arm around Ali's, dressed to the teeth for an evening with one of the firm's owners and partners, her direct superior. He had invited some friends to a dinner party in the southeastern suburb of Saltsjöbaden, where he owned a large villa directly on the shore, with exquisite views out into the Stockholm archipelago.

Anna knew him well; they had been friends long before he had interviewed her for her first position with his brand-new PR firm. They had originally met at a party with common friends in the city. Anders being a few years older than Anna, he had become a mentor of sorts. He and his husband Emilio were a bit eccentric, old-school DINKs, and art collectors. It was this latter capacity that provided the backdrop for tonight's dinner invitation. Anders had recently acquired a rather exclusive sketch by a famous Swedish artist, a piece that would change Swedish art history, or so he had claimed in his invitation. Whatever excuse Anders and Emilio needed to host guests was a welcome one.

Same, same, yet here I am, with a man at my arm. Some things do change after all. Anna chuckled, and Ali noticed.

"What's the matter?"

"Nothing, love. I was just remembering the last time I was here. Without you."

"Is there a problem?" Ali looked nervously at her. He was quite self-conscious about how a certain proportion of Sweden's population felt about the likes of him.

"No, not at all," Anna patted his hand, sensing what he was thinking. "Anders and Emilio are the opposite of racists. Emilio is Honduran, so he knows what it's like. They're progressive poster boys. It's just that I've never had a boyfriend to bring to one of their soirées before." Ali gave her a look. "Partner, sorry. We're past the adolescent stage." Her comment made her laugh again. "I guess it's just me. I never thought I'd fall for anyone long enough to change my self-perception of 'Anna, the eternal single.' Yet here we are." She pulled his hand to her lips and kissed it. "You make me happy!"

"I'm glad we are, and I'm glad I met you. You make me a better man every single day." Ali flashed her a smile that made her knees buckle. He was so sincere, and those eyes… She considered turning around and going straight back to the apartment, but Anders would never forgive her. Instead, she rang the doorbell.

"Anna!" Anders exclaimed when he opened the door. From the inside, she could hear dance music being played. Anders was dressed casually, as he normally was in his home, in jeans and a black turtleneck sweater. Emilio appeared at his side, flashing one of his trademark gleaming smiles. "*Bienvenidos!* How are you? Please, please, come on in. We've been expecting you." Emilio gently shoved his husband to the side to allow Anna and Ali to come in.

Emilio instantly chatted up Ali as he took his jacket and hung it in the hallway. "How do you like our house?"

Ali smiled. "Let's just say I've never been to a house where I had to take an elevator to get to the front door. It's unusual."

"*Sí*," Emilio replied, laughing. "We put that in a few years ago when Anders' mom was still alive. She hated going in on the ground floor, as it's more of a family and personal area with a gym, our in-house theater, and all the practical stuff like the laundry room and storage. She insisted on coming in through the main door, and that's up here. She also hated taking the stairs on the other side of the house, where the entrance was originally, so we decided to take advantage of the town building a new road and create a new entrance on this side, near the living room. It allowed us to renovate and do away with the old entrance altogether, which, incidentally, is where we have the best views of the bay. We replaced it with a window wall. Come on, I'll show you." Emilio pulled Ali along while Anders waited for Anna to take off her shoes.

"I'm so glad you could join us tonight. It's just a small gathering, and I wanted your opinion on how we could best handle the PR for the event."

"What do you mean?" Anna wasn't sure why he would need PR for a piece of art.

"The sketch has been preliminarily authenticated. It's a genuine Zorn. Can you believe it? When the art dealer told me, I was skeptical. I mean, an unknown Zorn, right? He's so famous! And even though there are hundreds of portraits and sketches he created, the likelihood of a new one popping up is infinitesimal. And to be able to buy it?"

"A lost Zorn? Are you serious?" Anna wasn't sure she did believe it. Like all Swedes, she was familiar with the Dalecarlian artist and had visited a huge retrospective at Sweden's National Museum just before the pandemic. Zorn was huge. His impressionistic style and the way he captured water were unsurpassed in Swedish art history. Or so Anna had always thought. She remembered being taken by her fathers to the local museum of arts in Gothenburg to view all the greats— the Picassos and Rembrandts—of the world, but there had also been a couple of paintings by Anders Zorn along with the museum's famous collection of Skagen paintings. They, too, were famous for the way they captured the very peculiar summer light in the Nordics.

That first Zorn painting had left an impression on Anna, and she had always loved how he was able to capture the reflection of sunlight on water. It was one of the most Swedish things she knew, the sun and the sea. Both were forever linked in the Swedish flag's blue and yellow.

Suddenly, she realized the implications. If Anders had truly gotten his hands on a hitherto unknown Zorn, that would be major news indeed.

"But what would you want to do with this? Spin it how?"

"That's where you come in, Anna. I want to make sure we don't appear greedy or…" He stopped for a moment to think.

"Or what?" Anna pressed.

Anders seemed to wriggle like a fish in a net. "I'm not sure. The history of this sketch is unknown. We bought it from a flea market in the countryside after it had been sold to them just recently."

"Okay. What's the problem?"

Anders shrugged. "Probably no problem whatsoever. But there's a lingering risk. When something priceless suddenly appears, it makes you wonder. Remember *Salvator Mundi*—the Leonardo painting—and how some people still think it's a fake?"

Anna nodded. She'd even seen the painting in Gothenburg when it was on global tour years and years ago.

"The guy who gave the preliminary confirmation is one of the foremost Zorn experts at the museum in Mora. He says it's genuine, but they need to take it in for additional verification. Zorn signed it but on the back, which is highly unusual."

"But if it is genuine and people already know about it…?"

"Well, one person knows. They've signed NDAs. In this case, it's not so much the authenticity I'm worried about but more the provenance."

"Meaning?"

"What if this wasn't from an estate but was stolen? Emilio and I were doing a drive through the countryside, as we do sometimes, looking for stuff, and we found this flea market near Enköping. It was one of these places where you can rummage on weekends and find trinkets.

"We found the sketch in a corner, and the seller was unaware of what it was. They had no record of the seller and said they hadn't paid a lot for it. They'd bought it because the motif appealed to the owner, the naked girl by the sea. Given it's a Zorn, that's not surprising." Anders laughed. "He had quite the reputation as a lady's man, and people used to tell stories in Mora claiming he'd fathered children all over the area. When I did some research into him, I was appalled by what a dirty old man he'd been."

Anna nodded. She'd heard about that side of Zorn. Male chauvinism in the arts was fairly common back then. Thinking of the #metoo movement, she corrected herself. *It still is!*

"When did you realize it was a Zorn?"

"The frame was so ugly, some cheap IKEA thing. I couldn't stand it, so we decided to put it into something nicer. That's when Emilio discovered the signature on the back. We took it to our regular arts dealer, who thought it looked genuine enough to get the experts in Mora involved."

"Wow, what a story. When can I see the piece? You're making me curious."

"After dinner. First, we eat. Then we will reveal it. We're still waiting for a couple of people to arrive." As Anders spoke, the doorbell rang again, and he went to welcome his business partner, Ove, and his wife Bella. They were the other founders and co-owners of the agency. They all hugged, and Bella handed Anders a bottle of Champagne.

"I presume we have something new to celebrate tonight? Your invite was rather cryptic. Hello, Anna. Good to see you. Are you feeling better? Is Ali here, too?"

"Yes, he is. Emilio kidnapped him and dragged him out to the front porch to see the view."

"Ah yes, he's a first-time visitor here, isn't he? I can understand the appeal. The boys have the perfect location. I prefer our little loft in the city, but to each their own."

Bella wasn't joking. She and Ove owned a huge condominium in the posh Östermalm neighborhood in downtown Stockholm, one of those old nineteenth-century apartments where rich people once lived and shared the space with their servants, all housed under one roof. Over the years, the apartment had been carefully renovated; the servant quarters had been converted into storage areas, laundry rooms, and walk-in closets, and a couple of rooms had been combined into larger bedrooms.

Bella's apartment was almost the exact opposite of Anders and Emilio's house, which had been built in the late 1990s on the site of an older summer home and was all open spaces, whitewashed walls, and large glass sections opening up to the Baltic Sea with spectacular views of the sunrise in the east, ships sailing past, and dark-green forest-covered islands all around. The house had a wide driveway and a private jetty where a sleek mahogany motorboat was moored.

Anders had bought the property about ten years ago, just after he and Emilio began dating. Anders' family had always been sort of wealthy, but even for him, at the time, it was a significant investment, and Anna remembered how nervous he'd been. In the years since, their agency had done very well, and today, Anders was a very wealthy man. *So much easier to become rich when you're born with money*, Anna thought with a sigh. It was a far cry from her youth. She was never poor, her fathers had always been decent earners, but their life had always been simple, centered around the island.

When Emilio and Ali returned from visiting the patio, they all sat down at the dinner table. As it was late in the fall, the sun had set a long time ago, and the only things visible in the darkness were the lights of homes across the strait and the odd vessel passing by a few yards from the house.

"What's for dinner?" Bella asked. "Making dinner for the little ones before leaving them in the care of the sitters has made me hungrier than I realized." She and Ove had ten-year-old twin girls. How they coped with running a large PR agency while raising twins, Anna had no idea. She barely coped with keeping her own life together.

"Emilio found a delicious piece of cod at the fishmonger's today. He's cooking it with fresh clams and a white wine sauce along with potatoes and vegetables. I hope you'll like it," Anders said as he served a small appetizer. "Just an *amuse bouche*. A trio of scallops on a wakame bed. Enjoy."

Meanwhile, Emilio served the white wine, a 2017 white Burgundy they'd found while touring the area the summer before the pandemic hit. It had a beautiful yellow color and was well paired with the seafood.

"Will you have some, too, Ali?" Emilio asked politely, not having met him before.

"Yes, please. I'm not religious." Ali blushed.

Anna smiled warmly at him. It must've been weird to him how some Swedes could be polite and considerate one minute and then completely inconsiderate the next. Anna had seen how the most blatant expressions of racism hid under the patina of consideration. She also knew her boss and his husband were not that kind of people. Emilio would never have forgiven himself if he'd served alcohol to someone who didn't drink, whatever the reason.

They ate their meal, chatting about this and that, commenting on the odd ship passing by, complimenting Emilio on the food, appreciating the wine, and talking politics. While their agency had "lost" the election because the party they had been working for had done badly at the polls, the campaign they had run had gathered a lot of goodwill for them, especially in professional circles. They had consequently attracted some new high-profile clients and were expanding—quite a challenge in the current environment with labor shortages everywhere, but it was a rather pleasant conundrum.

When they were finally done with their food and Emilio had served espressos to those who wanted one, accompanied by a fine grappa, Anders stood up and requested people's attention. Instantly, all conversation around the table died down, and everybody's eyes were on him.

"Friends," he began formally, "we asked you here because we have something big to show you." A grin spread across his face. "As you know, collecting art is a bit of a hobby of ours, and we recently made an exciting discovery." Turning, he gestured to the wall behind him where a veiled frame hung. Advancing on it, he carefully lifted the veil, revealing a slightly yellowed paper with a sketch of a young woman wading ankle-deep into the sea.

Anna's heart skipped a beat. The drawing was familiar somehow, but she wasn't sure why. It reminded her strangely of her mother, Lena. Perhaps that was it?

Aside from the young woman, there was a small boat pulled up on the beach off to one side and, in the background, the contours of small islands. It was a simple but beautiful sketch, charcoal on paper, but the longer Anna looked at it, the stronger her feeling that she'd seen it before.

"I, uh…I… God. I think I know this sketch. Or at least, I've seen a very similar one. How did you get this?"

Anders looked at Anna as if she'd said the most ridiculous thing ever and laughed loudly. "How could you possibly have seen it? It's been lost for over a hundred years."

Anna continued to stare at the drawing, memories coming to the fore of it—or a strikingly similar picture—hanging in her childhood home.

"I'm sorry, Anders. It's just that we had a drawing like this in our attic when I was younger. I am sure of it. I remember asking my parents about it and Pa telling me it was his great-grandmother. It used to hang in their bedroom, but Dad didn't like it, so they moved it to the attic. I haven't seen it in years, so you're probably right. I'm just mixing things up."

Anders' angry frown made it clear how much he disliked the direction the conversation had taken, and he swiftly moved on to explaining why this was such a unique find. Zorn normally didn't use a charcoal to draw, and it was quite unusual for him to sign it on the back. "The expert from Mora suggested it was likely a gift for a local girl he had a short dalliance with. He drew her but didn't want to make a big deal of it, as he was already well-known and may even have been married by then. He also didn't want to just renounce it, so he signed it on the back. That way, people would see it but they wouldn't see it was his. He was quite vain that way, was good old Zorn."

People got up from the table to admire the sketch, including Ali.

"It's stunning. Look at her face. So beautiful, so young." He looked back at Anna. "She reminds me a little of you." He laughed.

Anna approached the image. It *was* beautiful, and realizing it was a lost Zorn made her almost reverent before it. Still, she couldn't shake the eerie feeling that this was indeed the picture from her youth. Her dad would know.

"Mind if I take a picture of it?" she asked Anders and snapped one quickly. "For reference when we're working on the campaign," she added. Anders nodded, taking her at her word. She had so many questions but didn't want to embarrass herself in front of her boss. Besides, how could the sketch have made its way from Styrsö all the way up to Stockholm? It made no sense whatsoever. Yet Anna needed certainty, especially given everything else that had happened. Maybe this was connected to Pa's death? *No, that's impossible. It was an accident, after all.* But in her head, her subconscious was going haywire.

The evening continued as they eventually moved into the large living room from where they enjoyed the amazing views out into the archipelago, discussing the sketch and how to best make use of it to further the firm's reputation.

"You could gift it to the Zorn Museum," Anna suggested, not sure Anders would take the bait. "That way, it gets back to where it belongs, and we could spin the corporate social responsibility aspect?"

"I don't want to part with it quite yet. It's not just the money, but to be able to have a genuine, never-seen Zorn in your house is a real treat." Anders blushed a little at his admission, and Emilio squeezed his hand. "But you do have a point, especially given the piece's somewhat mysterious past. I'd hate for the police to show up here one day and claim it had been stolen." He wasn't done thinking about it. "Or have others tell me it's just one of many sketches. Who knows, maybe the one you remember is another Zorn sketch?" He looked at Anna for confirmation. She shrugged noncommittally.

Ove chimed in on the dubious provenance of the drawing. "If you're even the slightest bit unsure, you're better handing it over to the museum. Let them deal with any fallout. If it turns out it was stolen, they can always pay off the owner in a 'pity us we're just a poor museum' deal. If that happened while it was still in your hands, it would cost you dearly because a claimant could go after your personal wealth. Do this well with a big PR show around it, the media eats out of our hands, the sketch becomes famous, the museum attracts new visitors and you can deduct it from your taxes. This could be good for the company. I like Anna's take. Plus it shields you from any potential liability. What else do you know about the sketch's previous owner?"

"That's the problem." Anders threw his hands in the air. "We don't know anything. The girl at the flea market said the owner bought it from someone who claimed to have found it at a sale *after* an estate sale. So within months, it's gone from an estate to an anonymous buyer, and then to a flea market. The question is whose estate sale was it and how did it end up with those people in the first place? I'm not even sure I want to know."

"Sadly you may have no choice," Anna cut in. "People will ask questions. I find it odd that a Zorn just pops up like this, out of the blue."

"We go to flea markets all the time, buying all kinds of junk for next to nothing, and every time we do, I hope the owners don't know what they're selling. Don't get me wrong. I wish them well, but obviously, I hope to find a treasure they've overlooked because of their cultural ignorance. This time, we gambled and were rewarded."

"You mean you take advantage of them?" Bella chuckled.

"That is *one* way to look at it. I'd rather see it as a win-win. The flea market makes a small profit, too. It's not like they lose money on the things they sell. It's hardly my fault if they don't appreciate what's right under their noses. Besides, you can't expect buyers to go back and share profits after they've invested money to verify if something is valuable. We paid a lot of money to get that sketch verified."

"But you still believe it could've been stolen." Ali said out loud what most people in the room were thinking.

Anders shook his head. "No, I don't think so. Have you been to a flea market? They gather a ton of stuff over time. Most of the things they buy themselves at estate sales or other flea markets, but it's not unheard of for people to sell to them directly because they need the money. For all I know, the estate sale was a story concocted by someone who needed quick money. Stranger things have happened."

"Can't you go back to the flea market and ask them for a certificate or some kind of proof of purchase?"

"That's not how these people operate. These are often hobby markets, and they buy stuff for cash. I'm sure you've seen the signs when you travel through the countryside. They probably bought that sketch for a couple of hundred kronor and didn't think about it. Or it came in a box or whatever. Who knows?"

Bella nodded in agreement. "I have an aunt who loves to go to flea markets. It's still very much a cash business." She looked pensive. "May I ask how much you paid for the sketch?"

"Two thousand. It's a steal. The certificate of authenticity makes it worth a hundred times that, maybe even more. Zorn's etchings sell for different sums, from ten thousand and up. But as I said, this is the only known sketch made with charcoal. That alone makes it a one of a kind. You do the math in terms of monetary value."

"I don't think we'll get any further debating this." Ove raised his voice to make himself heard. "My suggestion remains. Donate it to the museum. Create a big fanfare, curate an exhibit—we could sponsor that, and who knows? Maybe after this is all done, they'll loan it to you or something if you so desperately want to see it every day." He seemed exasperated. "Or keep it here for all I care. But if you want to squeeze PR out of having discovered a Zorn without putting your home in the news and getting people to ask about its provenance, which they will, donating it to the museum in Mora is the best bet. Put a plaque with your names as donors underneath it, immortalizing you along with it. I'm sure our lawyers could draw up a donation contract that shields you from personal liability."

"And if I may be so bold," Bella added, "unique pieces like this belong in the public realm. While I can see the appeal of owning it, I don't think that's who you two *really* are." She smiled at both Anders and Emilio, sitting next to each other looking like scolded children.

Emilio nodded. "I'm glad you said that because that's how I feel, too. We've had quite a few discussions since we brought this home. Both of us know Zorn, of course. But we knew of his portraits, his paintings mainly. We had no idea how unique this is and what a crucial piece it could be in the puzzle to understand his life, his legacy. It is quite a remarkable piece."

Anna sat silently, observing the conversation. Now and then, she glanced over to the dining room and the wall where the drawing hung. It was small and she couldn't make out the details from a distance, but the more she saw it, the more convinced she became that it was the drawing that had once hung in her fathers' bedroom. She recognized that young woman's face, her nose. She'd have to ask Dad if he still had the drawing.

***

By the time the evening drew to an end, Anders and Emilio had decided to donate the drawing to the Zorn Museum in Mora. The firm's lawyer would draw up the contracts, and Anna would handle the PR aspects with the museum. She knew she also had to pursue the drawing's origin, and a text to her father would be the first step.

She sent him the photo of the drawing from the back of Ove's car—he'd offered them a ride back to the city—and froze momentarily when her father responded demanding to know what Emilie's drawing was doing in Stockholm.

Emilie's drawing?

Anna called him. "Dad?"

"It's late. When did you take that picture?"

"Tonight at my boss's house."

"That's impossible!"

"Well, then, tell me, when *did* I take the picture?"

"I don't know. But that's Lennart's great-great-grandmother Emilie. She used to hang above our bed. I hated her looking down on us at night!"

"I know, Dad. I remember," Anna said coolly. Did he really think... "Wait!" They had to be talking at cross purposes. "You think I took the drawing from the house and brought it up here to Stockholm?"

"How else did it get there?"

"I'd like to know that, too, which is why I sent you the photo— the one I took at my boss's house tonight?"

"Ah!" He laughed. "Well, there's quite the story behind that sketch. You could say it was the price a young man paid for being able to get his way with her."

"What do you mean?"

"It was a gift from an artist she had an affair with as a young girl. Back then, that was frowned upon, as you can imagine. She was just sixteen. Got pregnant, too. She was very much like your mother that way."

"So you're sure the drawing is the one from our house?"

"Of course I am! I took it down myself when we moved in. I stored it in the attic. It's still there."

"Are you sure?"

"As sure as I can be. I certainly haven't taken it down, and I doubt Pa would've. Why do you ask?"

"Because I wasn't joking when I said I took this photo today."

Tore didn't respond to that for a while. "Okay, I'll go check, but not now. It's late, and I'm already in bed. I'll call you in the morning."

"You don't have to do that. We're coming down to see you tomorrow, remember?"

"Oh, yeah, right. I forgot for a moment. Well, I'll let you go look then. God knows what it's like up there. I haven't been in the attic for quite some time. It'll be dusty and full of cobwebs, for sure. Remind me to tell you the full story of that drawing then, okay?"

"I will. Goodnight, Dad. See you tomorrow."

"Goodnight, dear."

– 23 –

October 29, 2022

As their train sped through the country, Anna smiled, watching Ali, who was mesmerized by the changing landscape of Sweden. She reflected on how this man had changed her life, as much as she had changed his. Subtly, he had nestled himself in her heart, with his gentle soul and his never-ending eagerness to help, completely oblivious to her deep distrust of relationships and her ingrained inability to love. He had somehow awakened something within her that she had never thought possible: to fall in love with someone. Or maybe she had not allowed anyone to make her feel this way before.

Her friends were all dumbfounded, too, by how queer, aromantic, freewheeling Anna Svensson had fallen for a man and devoted herself fully to a traditional, heteronormative relationship, a classic twosome—at least from their outside perspective, that was how it would look, and they were all wrong because Ali was anything but traditional. It had taken him only a little more than a five-hour trip from Stockholm to Gothenburg to fully embrace Anna and her rainbow family despite his upbringing and cultural roots.

Anna smiled again, thinking back to their video call with Ali's mother Haafiza a couple of weeks ago. He'd introduced Anna and then told her about Anna's fathers, and silence had descended. His mother did not approve of the sinful ways of the Swedish, their perceived looseness, morally, sexually, and otherwise. That he had chosen to move to Sweden rather than staying in Turkey or another Muslim country had put a real strain on Ali's relationship with his family and relatives back in Syria, and meeting Anna seemed to reinforce his mother's every preconception of Sweden. This "older woman" her son was dating had grown up in a family structure that was unfathomable, *and* she was still unmarried at her age?

Eventually, Ali's mother relented and accepted her son's choice, or so he said. His mother only spoke Arabic, and Anna did not. She'd need to work on that. She still wasn't sure what had caused Haafiza more offense, the fact that her son was dating a non-Muslim woman or that Anna's parents were gay. Ali hadn't mentioned that Anna was also queer. It wouldn't have helped. Not a bit. Anna had to chuckle at that and wondered to herself how it could be that she already thought of Haafiza as her mother-in-law. She quite liked the old woman with her vivid brown eyes that missed nothing. She must've been a striking beauty in her youth and still instilled a strong sense of respect in Anna. But some things were best left unspoken.

Mother-in-law. That implied marriage, a concept that had been utterly foreign to Anna just a couple of months ago. Now it seemed like the logical next step. But it would not be a big affair, no. They would go to City Hall at some point and get it over with. Or would Ali like a real wedding? She couldn't believe she was entertaining these thoughts. What had happened to her? Why had she changed so much? Had she always secretly longed for a relationship? Or had Ali's gentle influence gotten her to this point? Was it he who made her feel this way?

Engaging in a thought experiment, Anna pictured her best friend Sven and tried to imagine marrying him. The thought had crossed her mind many times over the years. After all, they had played a married couple as children. It hadn't been a pretty image then, and it still wasn't. As much as she loved him, as one would an annoying sibling, being married to him was not something she could envision. It just didn't work.

But replace Sven with Ali and this weird sense of domestic bliss reappeared—the two of them working side by side in the kitchen, making their meals together, showing him how to prepare some of her childhood dishes just as he would show her some of the wonders of Syrian cuisine. Cook together, eat, and clean up together.

Her heart beat faster at memories of snuggling up against him on the couch, his arm draped around her as they watched TV together, or getting ready for bed and the way he undressed, turning away bashfully, which only made her want him even more, not to mention their nights together and his unnerving ability to know exactly what got her juices flowing. Anna had to admit defeat. Ali was indeed her Waterloo. She had finally met her destiny, and never before had a defeat felt so amazing.

She put those thoughts to the side. The events of the previous night were still on her mind. That sketch, the face of the young woman, how it reminded her of her aunt—no, her mother. Lena. She'd have to make up her mind about how to refer to her. Mother felt wrong, but so did aunt. *Lena it is.*

It was eerie how much Lena looked like the girl in the sketch. Anna pulled up the photograph and zoomed into the girl's face. Yes, that was definitely the Svensson nose. But if that was true, then how did the sketch end up in that flea market? Had Pa sold it without telling Dad?

Or was something afoot? Had someone broken into the house and been discovered by Pa? No, that made absolutely no sense. Who would break into a house and leave wallets and an expensive phone but go into the attic to find a sketch?

Pulling into Gothenburg's central station, she was still none the wiser as to how the sketch had ended up in that flea market. She couldn't even be entirely sure that it was her great-great-grandmother. But what if it was?

– 24 –

October 29, 2022

THE WEATHER WAS glorious. Anna and Ali sat outside on the ferry's upper deck to enjoy the sunshine. Being back for the third time in just six weeks made Anna look at the houses lining Snobbrännan differently. The archipelago was so beautiful. How had she ever hated this place? Recently, the memories of her childhood had begun to feel like a bad dream, and the emotions they had always evoked faded into the depths of her subconscious, the pain of the memories slowly ebbing away.

The walk to the house was nice. They met a few tourists and neighbors who had been out on walks or grocery shopping, dragging their utility carts behind them. Some things never changed around here.

Tore was in the kitchen making lunch when they walked into the house.

"Dad? We're home." Home? Why had she chosen this term? Again. This hadn't been home in years. Yet it had felt right.

Tore came into the narrow hallway from the kitchen, carrying a towel and a large kitchen knife. "Welcome, dear." Looking at Ali standing behind Anna, he added, "It's good to see you again, Ali." He then clumsily hugged them both, trying to hold the knife away from them. "Sorry. I was chopping onions. Are you hungry?"

"Not really. We ate on the train. Look, I'm dying of curiosity here. Do you mind if we go upstairs and look for the drawing?"

"No, not at all. Go right ahead. I'll just finish up in the kitchen. Coffee?"

"Yes! That would be great." Anna smiled at him. "Come on," she said to Ali.

They climbed the stairs to the second floor and put their bags into her bedroom, then headed toward the narrow, steep staircase up to the attic. Anna put her foot on the bottom step and stopped.

"Are you okay?" Ali asked. "Do you want me to go up there first?"

"No, no, it's fine. I mean, I know we won't find Pa up there. The police searched the entire house, and Dad was up here, too, on the day Pa disappeared. I don't know. It's just a feeling I have."

"Premonition?"

"It's as good a word as any. To be perfectly honest, I'm afraid of what will happen if we don't find the drawing of Emilie. What would that signify?" Before Ali could answer, Anna's phone rang in her pocket.

"Yes, this is Anna Svensson."

"Anna, hi. This is Peter. I have news."

Anna felt her knees buckle. "Have you found something?"

"We have indeed. The divers had been busy and weren't able to get out into the search area until this morning. They dove at the coordinates where the finger was found, and..." He hesitated for a moment. "We've found Lennart's body. We'll run DNA tests, of course, but we're fairly sure it's Lennart, not only from the physical description you provided but also because the body was missing the right little finger, the one we'd already identified."

Anna couldn't shake the feeling that there was worse news to come. At the same time, she was fighting tears of relief that were trying to break past her eyelids. They'd finally found Pa. All of Pa.

Pa's dead.

"Okay. Thank you for this information. There's more, isn't there?"

"You're very perceptive. The way we found Lennart was quite unusual. Now, we can't jump to any conclusions, but he was found with an anchor chain tied around his waist and legs and an anchor attached to the other end. This rules out an accident, Anna."

"What are you saying? That he was murdered?"

"No, that's not what I'm saying. At least, not yet. There will need to be an autopsy, but it could also mean that he committed suicide. Have you heard of any missing boats on the island?"

Anna had to sit down on the stairs.

"What's going on?" Ali asked, worry written all over his face.

"They found Pa. Chained to an anchor on the seabed," she whispered to him before responding to the police officer, "I don't know. This is a lot to take in. Why would Pa do that? He had no reason to commit suicide, not that I know of. I'll need to talk to Dad about the boat. Maybe he's heard something. We have Facebook groups where people post about stuff disappearing. Usually, it's bicycles or the occasional golf car or moped, and they've told me about outboard engines being stolen, but an entire boat? I seriously doubt Pa would steal a boat to commit suicide. This just wouldn't be him. But I'll ask and call you back." She hung up and gave in to the tears, the emotions breaking free.

Tore came upstairs. "What happened? Why are you crying? Have you found something?"

Ali took the old man and guided him into his bedroom. Anna followed them like a robot.

"Here, Tore, sit down. Anna just had a call from the police. They found your husband's remains, chained to the seabed. They say it might have been suicide."

Tore stared incredulously at Ali and Anna. "They what? But that makes no sense. Why would Lennart kill himself? We were happy!" He almost screamed out the final words.

"Dad, calm down. We don't know yet. They'll have to perform an autopsy first."

"But why? I...I can't believe that Lennart would do that to me."

"Well," Ali said gently, "we can't be sure until the autopsy is done. There are other possibilities."

Tore looked up in confusion at the man who'd captured his daughter's heart. "What do you mean?"

"He might have been killed."

Almost hateful, Tore responded. "That's preposterous! Complete nonsense. Why would anyone kill my Lennart? He was the kindest, gentlest man on the entire island. He wouldn't have hurt a fly, so why would anyone hurt him? That's just not possible."

"Dad, I know," Anna said. "Ali isn't saying Pa *was* killed, just that the police aren't ruling it out, that's all. They have to pursue all avenues. But you have to admit that the anchor chain puts things in a very different perspective."

Tore was crying. "Lennart, Lennart, what did you do?"

Anna got up and hugged her father before turning to Ali with a renewed sense of purpose—and a weird feeling that made the hairs on her nape prickle. "Could you look after Dad for a while? I'll go upstairs to see if I find the drawing."

Ali nodded to say he would.

Anna climbed the steep staircase, opened the narrow wooden door to the attic, and turned on the light—a bare bulb hanging by a cord from the roof that gave off a cold, bright-white light. She had to stop looking at it to see anything else around her. After a few moments, her eyes adjusted to the conditions, and she began to search for the drawing. Someone had recently shifted furniture around up here and cleared some space right behind the door. She moved around the attic, looking at old commodes and dressers, but no drawing was hiding anywhere, not inside any cupboard or drawer. There were also a number of old cardboard banana boxes; she opened the first one and rummaged through its contents.

"Anna? Are you okay?" Ali's voice came from directly behind her.

"Yeah. How's Dad?"

"He's lying down for a while. I think the news was too much for him. Have you found anything?"

"Not yet. I've checked through all the furniture. The old banana boxes are next."

"Banana boxes?"

"Yeah, we used them when we moved here, you know, before moving boxes were a thing?" She shook her head. "But somehow, I can feel it in my bones that the drawing is missing. It's too big to fit in these boxes, what with the frame and all. You saw it at Anders and Emilio's place, right? It was like an A3, pretty big. Then again, if my memory was wrong and 'our' sketch is still here, maybe it was smaller. Wanna help me? We need to go through all these boxes." Anna pointed to a pile of around twenty banana boxes, neatly stacked one on top of the other.

They worked for a good three hours, searching through every box, every corner of the attic, but they didn't find the drawing.

"If that drawing in Stockholm really is ours, how on earth did it end up there?"

Anna called the police and let them know about her find or lack thereof. Naturally, the inspector wasn't convinced.

"Well, it is quite the story, but at this point, that's all it is. A story. We need the autopsy to make sure our next step is based on facts and not assumptions. I'll call you as soon as we have the results."

– 25 –

October 29, 2022

TORE HAD BEEN to Donsö to buy fresh fish, which, despite Ali's offer to cook, he insisted on preparing for dinner. Anna had gone out for a walk to clear her head and try to make sense of the missing drawing of her great-great-grandmother. She didn't seem able to let go of the coincidental appearance of a masterpiece by the great Anders Zorn and the disappearance of her father, and there was nothing Ali could say or do to make her feel better. He'd gotten to know her well enough to understand that there were things she needed to figure out for herself.

While Tore was busy over the stove, Ali moved around the kitchen table, putting down plates and utensils, and he and Tore made easy conversation. Tore was more than curious about Ali and how he had mysteriously captured his daughter's heart.

"You've known each other a month now, haven't you? And you've already moved in with each other?" Tore chuckled. "I never thought it would be possible for anyone to capture my daughter and sweep her off her feet like that. What's your secret?"

"I'm not sure I follow," Ali said.

"Anna made it abundantly clear to Lennart and me—and anyone else who'd listen, for that matter—that she was not interested in relationships. At all. She always said she was happy by herself, with her friends, and just enjoying sexual encounters and having flings. She certainly never introduced anyone to us." He barely looked up as he said this, just smiling and shaking his head, stirring the béchamel sauce he was working on. "And you showed up before you even became an item. Maybe that was the trick."

"I don't know. As you say, I haven't known her that long, and for what it's worth, I wasn't looking for a relationship either. Where I come from, these things are usually planned and not taken lightly. To just fall for someone, while not unheard of, is one thing, but a relationship requires careful planning. Families are involved, and you need to be able to support your future bride and prove it to her parents." Ali shrugged. "I know it's not like that here." He made a circling gesture with his free hand. "Anna makes more than enough money by herself. She doesn't need me to support her. Sweden is so different."

"The only thing that matters is that you found each other and fell in love, right?"

"Yeah. We did. I don't even know when it happened. There was something about her, this inexplicable vulnerability paired with her strength and determination in this crisis."

"I'm not complaining. Maybe you've heard from Anna, but we haven't always been close. In fact, it wasn't until Lennart's disappearance that we even began to talk to each other instead of yelling. In the past, my texts or voicemails could go unanswered for weeks, and she mostly talked to Lennart. I don't blame her. I was not a terribly good father to her."

"She's mentioned you two didn't get along," Ali said tactfully. "May I ask why that is?"

"It's a long story. I'm sure we'll get to talk about it at some point in more detail—when Anna is with us. I'd rather not exclude her point of view from this conversation. I don't want to make things any worse than they already are. But in short, I was obsessed with keeping up appearances. Being a young, gay couple out here in the eighties was very difficult, and I think I made Anna inadvertently bear the brunt of it all. With hindsight's wisdom allowing me to see things differently, I can't blame her for getting out of there as quickly as she could."

"I'm still getting used to how openly you live," Ali admitted. "This would be quite impossible in Syria. I don't think I know any gay people back home, although I might suspect one or two, given what I've seen here in the past few years."

"Things here have changed dramatically in the years since the AIDS pandemic broke out. I'm not sure if it was just that the government wanted us gays out of public restrooms and parks, but after civil unions were introduced for gay couples in 1994, things moved at a very rapid pace. Today, nobody bats an eyelash when a gay couple gets married. That's an amazing accomplishment, yet there is still work to be done, abroad and here, too."

"How did you and Lennart meet?"

"Hah! That was inevitable. We both grew up here on the island. Mind you, he was five years my senior, and we were never part of the same circles, but we knew of each other. And I guess we realized, at some point, that we were both the same. You know, friends of Dorothy. There had, of course, always been gay people on the islands, but we had to hide it to survive just as everyone else did. Maybe more so in a small community such as ours, where you spent most days on the island until secondary school. Only then did we have to take the ferry to the closest school in town. That was also a time when many of us dropped out of school after the mandatory nine years, to take up work as sailors or fishermen. Only those who wanted to become officers moved on to high school and college."

"That doesn't sound very romantic."

Tore laughed. "No, it wasn't romantic. The first time we spoke to each other, we were hanging out, you know the way kids do? I was there with friends of mine, at Bratten, with our bikes and mopeds, smoking, talking. We'd drive mindlessly around the island and usually stop by the harbor to see the ferry coming in from town. Back then, there wasn't as much evening traffic as today, and we hoped we might know someone we could ask for a cigarette or who would buy booze for us in town and deliver."

"Lennart was a pusher?" Ali asked, shocked.

"No, not at all, but as he was older than we were, he was the perfect object of our adulation. While my friends hoped that he might give them a cigarette to share, I was mesmerized by his beauty. He was so tall, and his blond hair hung shoulder length even back then. I don't remember exactly what happened, but I don't think he had any cigarettes. Lennart never smoked, and I think my friends were mocking him because of it, calling him names, including the F-word."

"F-word?" Ali wondered.

"Faggot, poof, you name it. I just remember the pain in his eyes, how hurt he was. But more so, I remember the way he looked at me, maybe hoping that I might say a kind word or stop my friends. He understood that I was gay, too, but at the time, I hadn't come out, let alone accepted who I was. But seeing his pain, and knowing in my innermost self that my friends and I were taunting not only Lennart but me, too, was getting to me. When he walked off to go home to his parents, I told my friends I needed to get home, too. After Lennart had turned the corner and wasn't visible anymore, I set out after him, and after catching up, we began to talk. I apologized, and he forgave me. Lucky me."

"How old were you?"

"Oh, I don't remember. Sixteen, seventeen? This was very early in the seventies. Lennart was going to college at the time, so he would've been old enough to peddle alcohol to us if he'd wanted to. Calling him out for being gay didn't earn us any favors."

"What was it like to date back then for you guys? Was it very difficult?"

"Oh my, you have no idea. We had to be so very careful. Nobody could know. This was also before either of us was out to our parents. But you know how kids are. They can smell blood, and when they call you gay, and they see how it stings, it sticks, regardless of whether there's any truth to it. Words like these are spoken long before people realize their true meaning.

"Lennart and I used to meet up in secret. We had our private retreat on the island. It's actually on a spot of land that his parents own, but I didn't know that at the time. Completely worthless, it is. Too small to build on, having been split again and again as it's been passed down from generation to generation. My friends took their girls over to Brännö Husvik for the weekly dances, but we couldn't go there, so we hid together. We got to know each other, and I think maybe it was the isolation, the loneliness of our existence back then, that created the strong bond that lasted for so long. Now that was quite romantic, come to think of it, the two of us, holding hands, looking out over the island toward Vinga and the open sea."

"That's both a sad and a beautiful story, Tore. Thank you for sharing it with me. I had never met gay people before coming to Sweden, not to my knowledge, and I feel ashamed for some of the prejudice I held. Anna gave me quite the lecture on our first ride down here."

"Did she now?" Tore chuckled. "That sounds like my daughter, all right."

"So you've been a couple for fifty years?" Ali said and let out an impressed whistle.

"Almost, yes. We didn't become a couple until I moved away from Styrsö in 1973. We would've celebrated our golden anniversary next year." The sadness in Tore's voice was palpable. "Not that it counts because we weren't able to get married until 2009."

"Did you get married?"

"No, not like that. We did enter a civil union when that became available to us in 1994. Back then, it was mostly for economic and legal reasons, you know? To provide Anna with the safety and stability we needed as a family. Lennart and I had been together for so long already that we didn't need the government to tell us it was the two of us. We had already arranged for all the paperwork and written our wills. When the law finally changed and allowed us a 'full' marriage, we simply applied for the upgrade, which we received on a computer-printed form months later. Very Swedish in a way."

"I can't even begin to imagine how that must've been."

"No, I guess you can't. And I'll be honest, it is sometimes difficult to remember, even for me, since so much has changed. When I left Styrsö to live my true life in the city, I moved in with Lennart in his student apartment. He was studying to be an engineer at Chalmers. He had done his military service and was in his second year. We lived together in this tiny studio during the first weeks before he was able to secure something bigger. I had begun to work at sea, on a cargo vessel, as a sailor, and I was gone for weeks at a time. I guess that's how we survived because otherwise, we might've gotten on each other's nerves." The memory made Tore chuckle. "When I came home, I'd be stuck in that tiny studio for weeks on end, and it drove us both crazy. So I voluntarily took on longer tours. I also managed to get out of the military service, as I was in the merchant fleet. Lennart graduated from Chalmers in 1975 and got work for an engineering firm in town, and I kept working at sea.

"You see, we couldn't get an apartment together, so it was his name on the lease. The landlord knew, of course. It was okay in a big city like Gothenburg, or tolerated, anyway. We moved back to Styrsö in 1985 when my in-laws passed away and left us the house. Anna was barely four at the time, and we were feeling crowded in the city, what with a child in a one-bedroom apartment. She needed her own space, and we felt that the island was the perfect place to raise a child."

"What was it like to move out here again? Given everything you said before?"

"It wasn't easy, I'll tell you that. There was a lot of resistance, from young and old. The school was okay, and we tried our best not to let Anna feel anything. But I guess she still did. Kids can be so cruel, but she was such a trooper and never said anything to us. We simply assumed, given the things Lennart and I had been through."

"Did you ever regret having her?" Ali wondered.

"No. How could we? Besides, that wasn't ever a choice. It's not like we walked into a supermarket and came home with a child that we could return. Lena made that choice for us, in a way, refusing to give up her daughter for adoption. It's tragic, really. She could still have come home and been the cool aunt, but she chose not to. I guess even giving Anna up to her brother was too much for her in the end."

"It's so sad," Ali said.

"And all for the sake of keeping up appearances." Tore shrugged but then laughed. "You should've seen the expression on Lennart's parents' faces when we went to see them the first time with Anna. They had no idea. They knew about me, of course, and it was hard enough for them to tolerate me, but when we walked up to the front door with a pram, they emerged, faces ashen, mouths wide open. It was a difficult visit, and they made it clear they didn't want us to keep the child, insisting it would bring misery and unhappiness to the family, not to mention that two men were utterly incapable of raising a child." Tore shook his head.

"We left the house after less than an hour and roamed the island for a while before we were able to catch a ferry back into the city. We didn't hear from them for months and then suddenly, one Sunday, they showed up at our door. After that, they slowly came around. They adored Anna. Sadly, as you know, they died in a car crash when she was still little. I'm not sure she remembers much about them."

"What about your parents?"

"There's not much to tell. My dad died at sea when I was still a child—he was also in the merchant fleet—and my mother died from cancer a few weeks before I graduated. We didn't have much money and lived in an apartment in Halsvik, above another family."

"I'm so sorry to hear that." While Ali knew from his own experience what it meant to lose family, he had not been close to his father due to his drinking, but he did miss his brothers, even though they'd been much older. And he missed his mother. The thought of losing her at such a young age was inconceivable.

He still relied on her counsel, even though they only spoke to each other on the phone every two weeks or so.

"She'd been ill for so long," Tore said. "You get to the point when death comes as a welcome guest. I was only eighteen when she died, and I joined the merchant fleet because I needed to make money. Lennart and I had met a couple of years earlier, and I sometimes stayed with him when getting off the ship. Eventually, I stopped coming back to Styrsö and the apartment. It just made no sense, and it was a painful reminder. The landlord looked after any mail, invoices, and stuff for me, but it felt as if I'd overstayed my welcome. I thought I'd never return to the island, but Styrsö has an almost magical pull on you. Once you set foot out here, you enter a different world. The pace is very different from that in town—I guess I always missed it. And over the years, the island has been very good to us.

"It is a beautiful place. So much water... It feels like paradise sometimes."

"And you've not yet seen what it's like here in the summer. The sun—oh Ali, you need to be here for the sunshine. Take an evening dip down in Halsvik, enjoy the sunset, or swim in the middle of the night around Midsummer, when it never completely darkens. It's often too cold to swim, but to just sit by the water, listening to the seagulls and the waves coming ashore. Man, I'm telling you, it almost makes you religious."

"I'll make sure we come out here then." As Ali said those words, Anna came back from her walk. "How are you, Habeebti?"

"Better, I think. I'm still none the wiser about the drawing, but I guess things will work out once the police are done with the autopsy."

They sat down and ate their dinner, making conversation about the weather, summers on Styrsö, and childhood memories from here and in Syria. Tore had fried the cod in butter, making sure the temperature wasn't too high or else it would become rubbery and not as tender as it could be, he said, and served it with cooked potatoes, green peas, and béchamel sauce. It was a simple yet delicious meal.

"Dad, you said you'd tell me the story of the drawing and Nana Emilie?"

Tore smiled. "I did, didn't I? I only know what Lennart told me and what Grandma Astrid knew. This all happened such a long time ago. Who knows what is legend and what is true?"

"Don't keep us waiting. What's the story?

Tore rolled his eyeballs upward as if that would help him remember. "Let me see. Nana Emilie was born in the second half of the nineteenth century, I don't remember the exact year, but when she was sixteen, she worked at the recently built restaurant at Styrsö Bratten where she met this young painter. The story goes that she fell in love and they spent an afternoon together out here somewhere, doing things that were considered inappropriate by society back then, at least for someone who was yet to be married. As a thank-you, he drew a sketch of her and gave it to her before he took the ferry back into town. She never saw him again."

Anna was pensive. "I remember Pa telling me this story a few times. She was his great-great-grandmother, right?"

Tore's forehead wrinkled as he did the math. "Let's see. Astrid, your grandmother, was born in 1931. Her mother's name was Gudrun, and she was still alive when I was younger. She must've been born around the turn of the century. But Gudrun wasn't Emilie's daughter. If I remember correctly—and you can always go and look it up in the church's records—Elsa was the name of Emilie's daughter. Her father died in a storm shortly after she was born, and they left the island to take up residence on Fotö where he was from. After his death, Emilie stayed on Fotö, as she didn't want to return to Styrsö and face all the gossip about her."

"Did Elsa come back?"

Tore nodded. "I believe so, yes, but I couldn't tell you when. You should go and visit the cemetery. They're all buried there somewhere."

"Do you think it's possible that Anders Zorn was that young artist?" Anna was thinking, trying to remember the portraits of Zorn she had seen. She couldn't and had to google to bring up one of his self-portraits. "I remember seeing this one at the national museum in Stockholm. Look, Dad, look at his nose. Does that remind you of the Svensson nose?"

Tore took Anna's phone and studied the image on the screen. "I don't know, dear. It looks just like a regular nose to me. Besides, you have Emilie's nose, and she certainly wasn't related to Zorn."

Ali chimed in. "Does this Zorn have any living heirs? Maybe you could get a DNA test done to see if you're related to him. It would make your story even more unique and give you answers about your heritage, at least on your mother's side."

Anna took her phone back and googled some more. "No, it's just as I recalled. Zorn and his wife never had any children, and if memory serves me, he never acknowledged any other kids either, although there were plenty of rumors that he'd impregnated half the women in and around the town of Mora at the time. No luck here either."

Tore put his hand on Anna's. "Don't worry about it. If you're interested in your family heritage, why not buy one of those DNA kits? That way, you can find relatives you didn't even know existed, not just the extended family here on the island. You might even find your biological father."

Anna frowned, "I'm not sure that's such a great idea. What if he's not a nice person?"

"Well, he was nice enough for Lena to be with him. I didn't know her very well, but she was a good girl. Kind, with a big heart. I doubt she'd have fallen for a bad apple."

The conversation began to drift away from Emilie and the sketch. It was nice to learn a little bit more about it and refresh her memory.

"Do you think it is possible that Lennart took his own life?" Tore wondered aloud after they'd cleared the plates and were doing dishes.

"I don't know, Dad. I really don't. I just can't see any reason why he would. I know you two didn't always see eye to eye, but I also know how much he loved you. I just can't fathom why he would do something so drastic, and this would've been totally out of character. He wasn't depressed or ill, was he?"

"No, not that I know of—unless he's been very good at keeping secrets from me, which I don't think he was. He had back problems, but he was in his seventies, after all. His blood pressure was fine. I remember he'd been to a checkup just recently at the clinic over in Bratten, and the doctor was pleased with his health."

"Which leaves us with the even more unlikely scenario of a murder," Ali said. "Can you imagine any scenario in which anyone would want to kill him?"

Tore merely stared at him, shaking his head. "I can't. This isn't Hisingen or the city, where they shoot each other in those gang wars. I mean, we've had a few incidents over the decades with people doing stupid things, and yes, there have also been suicides out here, people drowning themselves. But we have no valuables in this house, no money."

Anna interrupted the darkening conversation. "Look, guys, there's no point in speculating. We'll simply have to wait and let the police do their part. Let's not jump to conclusions."

***

They spent Sunday walking around the island. "Since when do you go for walks?" Anna was amused at the fact that Dad had begun walking.

"Ever since Lennart disappeared, I have been out here a lot. Because I know that he worked on these hikes, it makes me feel closer to him somehow. The guys at the Pathfinders have been inviting me to their meetings, too. They're very kind, and everybody is looking out for me."

Tore wanted to show Ali some of these sights and the trails that Lennart had been a part of in setting up and maintaining. Ali had particularly enjoyed Urbers stig, the latest of the trails the Pathfinders had put in order. As they walked across the little wooden bridges over what would be small streams of water in the spring but were currently dry beds, Anna felt that same connection to Pa her dad had talked about. Somehow, here, he would be present for as long as he would be remembered.

They walked past Gläntan, a small shelter built by local scouts, before the trail connected back to the main network of paths. They had to walk up past Sundkällan, which had once been used for open-air concerts.

"This is such a beautiful place," Ali remarked.

"It is," Anna agreed. "All things considered, I had a good childhood." She looked at her father, who smiled fondly. "Growing up out here is idyllic and in many ways unique and beautiful. You're as safe as a child can be. But it's also a small environment where everybody knows everybody. Sticking out from the crowd isn't easy, and conformity is valued. I was sometimes bullied in school, not so much for who I was but because of who my parents were. Do you remember, Dad?"

Tore nodded sadly. "I'm so sorry. Had we known you would have to go through all that, we'd have stayed in the city."

Anna shook her head. "No, Dad. Never ever take the blame for other people's ignorance. First of all, you didn't do anything wrong in the way you raised me. I had my own room and clean clothes, and there was always food and plenty of love in our house. You were great parents—you still are. You can't take the blame for others thinking you aren't fit to raise a child. I know both you and Pa did everything you could to keep me sheltered and to minimize the hurt I felt." She shrugged. "But no parent can forever shield their children from the world's cruelty."

"It's hard to conceive when you look at Sweden today," Ali said. He had trouble reconciling the Sweden he had gotten to know with their accepting attitudes with how different it had been just twenty years ago. "What happened to you?"

"Oh, just verbal abuse mostly. Sometimes my classmates would ask me what it was like living in the same house as 'those gays,' whether my fathers would have sex while I was watching, that sort of stuff. Which is completely crazy, of course. I'm not sure if they had caught their own parents doing it on the weekend or if they genuinely thought gay people were aliens with a completely different way of doing things." She laughed. "Seriously though, it was the fact that they never stopped. These questions began when I was in elementary school and continued up into high school."

"I remember some of it," Tore chimed in, "but I think you kept a lot to yourself. I'm sorry you felt that you couldn't be more open with us, and I carry a lot of guilt for my methods to shield you from the abuse." He paused to greet a neighbor, who passed them with her dog. "Hello, Rufus!" He petted the dog on the head, and the animal jumped up, eagerly wagging its tail. "You're such a good boy." Looking at the owner, he smiled. "I hope all is well with you?"

Anna watched the exchange with interest. "I didn't know you liked dogs. Maybe you should get one, too? To keep you company?"

Tore shook his head. "One thing at a time, dear. Let's not get carried away."

They walked on, passing the local pet supply store on their way back to the house, and as Tore waved at Kattis, the owner, he added with a sad voice. "I wish I'd known what it would do to us, listened more to you back then, dear. I'm sorry for that."

"Water under the bridge," Anna said and took her dad's hand. "Has this been here long?"

"What?" Tore wasn't sure he understood.

"The pet supply store."

"Yeah, a few years. I think a lot of people appreciate not having to carry all those cans and bags with pet food from the city."

"My friends and I used to go to concerts and parties here," Anna told Ali. "A bunch of local youths brought in bands from Gothenburg and beyond. It was fun for several years, but the organizers grew older, and there were a couple of incidents with stolen boats after visitors had missed the last ferry, after which it fizzled out. But I remember getting quite drunk here."

"I remember that, too," Tore said. "I also remember how much trouble you were in afterward."

Anna shrugged. "Yes, Dad, I know. I was there. There wasn't much else to do out here when I was a kid. Is Öhålan still the only place where kids can hang out?"

"Yes, and they still do—driving around, vandalizing mailboxes and trash containers, and then some."

Anna explained for Ali's benefit. "There's this youth club, run by the city, called Öhålan, but it's only open to kids of a certain age group, and it's not open every day and not very late. Several parents out here don't want their kids to be at home with their friends, being loud and disturbing the adults. So they're outdoors all hours of the night, driving around on their mopeds, and, well, you do the math. Bored as they are, they challenge each other, playing dare, and the group pressure is immense. Been there, done that."

Tore sighed. "Some things never change. The damage they cause runs into hundreds of thousands of kronor, and they're completely oblivious to the consequences to others. Golf carts are dumped in the ocean, and just a year ago they destroyed the restrooms at the Bratten marina, pouring concrete into the toilet bowls."

Anna shook her head. "I know I wasn't God's best child, but I never destroyed anything. I couldn't do that to you. Things were difficult enough for you as they were. I didn't want to make it worse." She looked at Tore, who wiped a tear from his eyes, and she took his hand. He smiled at her.

"Looks like we didn't screw up completely as parents then, eh?"

– 26 –

November 1, 2022

Aᴺᴺᴀ ᴀᴺᴰ Aʟɪ had returned to Stockholm late on Sunday night. It had been a good weekend, and she hadn't felt this close to her father in a long time, but they both had work to return to.

Anna had promised she'd look into Ali getting a medical license in Sweden. She knew his family was trying to recover the records of his qualifications locally in Aleppo, but it was an arduous process, assuming the paperwork had survived the countless bombings of the civil war in the first place. There had to be another way. It was a shame to waste his talents on driving cars and doing odd jobs to scrape a living when Sweden was screaming for more doctors. But without his university transcripts readily available, it wouldn't be easy and would take time. Perhaps there was another way for Ali to validate his knowledge and be admitted to the fast-track course. Anna didn't know, but she had friends in high places who would.

The phone call from the police didn't come as a surprise. Nevertheless, the finality of it made her hesitate to answer the call.

"Peter, hello. I presume you have news for me?"

"Anna, hello. Yes, I do indeed, and I'm afraid it's not good news."

Anna instinctively slumped in her office chair.

"I'm sorry," the inspector said. "I guess all news coming from me is bad news at this time. I just heard from pathology, and they confirmed that Lennart did not die from natural causes. His neck was broken. There are also signs of blunt force trauma to the back of his head. Our working theory now, therefore, has to be that someone killed him."

Lost for words, the sound that escaped Anna was a mix between a groan, a gargle, and a scream.

The inspector gave her a moment before he continued. "We will have to go back to the interviews we conducted in September and see if we find any clues as to what might have happened that day. This is now a murder investigation, and you can rest assured that we will find whoever did this to your father."

Anna's head was spinning. Her thoughts and emotions were all over the place, and she couldn't focus or grasp on to any of it. She tried to think who might've had a reason to kill Pa. Someone he knew? No. He got on with everyone. A stranger then. But why? What would they stand to gain? *The lost Zorn...* "Do you think this could've been about the drawing?"

"Yes, absolutely. If the killer realized its value, it would provide a clear motive, which brings me to the other reason for my call. Do you have the phone number of the people who purchased the drawing? We need to talk to them and see what they can tell us."

"I'll text you Anders Norén's direct number."

"Thank you. You don't happen to know where they purchased it or from whom?"

"No. I think they mentioned a place in Enköping?"

"Okay, we'll follow up on that. Meanwhile, please keep this to yourself, at least for now. I understand you'll want to tell your father, but we don't want to give the murderer an opportunity to do away with any evidence. In these kinds of cases, the killer is usually found among people nearby."

"You're not accusing my dad, are you?"

"No, although we can't entirely rule that out either. He certainly is a person of interest."

"Dad recently told me about being accosted by a bunch of homophobic kids."

"Are you saying he might be in danger, too?"

"I don't know, but you should talk to him."

"We will, I promise. Will you tell him about our findings, or shall we?"

"No, no, I'll do it. But you'll keep us posted on the progress of the investigation?"

"Of course. I'm sorry for the bad news."

After the call ended, Anna got up and walked to the window of her office, overlooking the Baltic Sea. Right in front of her was Skeppsholmen with its museums and the youth hostel *AF Chapman*, an old schooner, moored in front of it. It was so familiar to her now, yet she missed the view that Pa had loved so much, from Salskärs Udde out west, the open sea. Here, all she could see were islands, buildings, and the odd vessel. As beautiful as it was, it was nothing like home.

Home!

She picked up her phone and dialed Dad's number. He answered after a couple of rings.

"Anna? How are you?"

"Dad. I've been better. I just got off the phone with the police. Are you sitting down?"

"No, I'm at Konsum. I needed some groceries. What is it? Is the autopsy done already?"

"Yes." She didn't know how to continue. She pictured her father standing in the aisles of the local cooperative, surrounded by neighbors and members of staff restocking shelves. On the one hand, giving him the news right there seemed more brutal somehow. On the other hand, if she didn't, it was also telling.

Tore put two and two together and whispered into the phone, "He was killed, wasn't he?"

"Yes, Dad. I'm sorry."

He didn't say anything for a while, and when he eventually spoke, his tone was flat. "I need to go. Let's talk later, okay?" Then he hung up, leaving Anna staring out the window, across the bay, this particular place where the arms of the Baltic Sea reached out to embrace Lake Malar.

– 27 –

November 21, 2022

A NNA NEEDED TO focus on work rather than the investigation of her father's murder. A few weeks had passed since she received the call about the autopsy results, and she still could neither believe nor comprehend that anyone would want to kill him. She'd spoken to the inspector several times, one of those being a formal interview as part of the investigation. She'd been ruled out as a suspect, and the rest of their communications were about trying to get information on their progress.

The inspector told her they were following several lines of inquiry, including the missing sketch and the recent attack on Dad, the latter of which they quickly dismissed as a prank by kids who didn't understand any better. They had questioned them and referred them to social services. As money often played a role in murder cases, they had cast a wider net and were looking into financial reasons as well. So far, it seemed they had lots of theories but little else to go by.

It was driving Anna mad, and work was the only thing keeping her from obsessing...which wasn't entirely true because she was still obsessing. Not a waking moment passed without her trying to make sense of the senseless. Who had killed her father? Why? Had it been an accident? Was Dad involved? If so, why go to such great lengths to hide the corpse? Fear of punishment? No, there had to be another reason behind this. Someone had killed her father deliberately, to accomplish something. But what? They weren't rich; her father had retired long ago and had little to no money to his name. The house they lived in was old, and while it was comfortable and welcoming, it was nowhere near a beach and thus would never sell for millions to rich summer guests from the city.

So why? Who wanted him dead? Nobody stood to profit from Pa's death, as everything he owned would go directly to Dad. Such were the inheritance laws when there was no will to stipulate otherwise. As long as Dad was alive, he'd get the house. There was nothing else.

The buzzing sound of her phone going off on her desk stirred her from reveries, and she smiled when she saw who was calling, though her troubled mind soon strayed to darker thoughts.

"Ali, is something wrong?"

"Habeebti, why would anything be wrong? I just wanted to check in with you, make sure you're okay. You were awfully quiet when you left this morning."

The effortlessness with which Ali had nestled into her life still baffled Anna. She, who had never been able to form lasting relationships, was so thankful for his steady presence in her life.

"Yeah, I know. Things have been crazy around here since the election. I need to focus if I want to have a job tomorrow."

Ali laughed. "From what I've seen, that's not how things work here in Sweden. They can't just fire you like that."

Anna laughed, too. "Ignore me. I'm just throwing myself a pity party. With everything going on in my life, the crazy workload is the icing on the cake."

"It's not all bad, is it?" Ali asked hopefully.

"No, it's not." Anna blushed at the thought of how much she'd come to love this man. "Look, I have a meeting in a few minutes. I need to get going. Talk more tonight?"

"If you want to?"

"Silly you! Of course I do."

"Good, I'll have dinner ready. Six o'clock?"

"Perfect! Thanks, I appreciate it." She pressed the red button to disconnect the line, then placed her palm on the screen as if touching Ali's face by proxy. She felt this warm fuzzy feeling every time she thought about or spoke to him. She had fallen in love with the man. *How crazy is that? Me falling in love is like snow falling in the Maldives.*

Her reveries were again interrupted by another call, this time from the generic 010 area code often used by public agencies. She picked up the phone and answered. "This is Anna Svensson."

"Anna, good morning. This is Peter Gustavson from the police in Gothenburg. Do you have a moment?"

"Hello, Peter. Not really. I'm about to walk into a meeting. Is it urgent or can I call you back?"

"No, not urgent at all. Just a discovery we've made during the investigation."

"Oh, color me intrigued. Tell me." Suddenly, she didn't care about being late for a staff meeting.

"We've discovered your father owned property on Styrsö. Did you know that?"

"Property? You mean besides the house Dad still lives in?"

"Yes. There are hundreds of plots on the island, some large, some small, and your father is registered as the owner of a couple of them. Mostly forest land, but one plot is sizable. You didn't know anything about it?"

Anna was perplexed. "Yeah, sorry. I did know about that, but it's all worthless. Did you speak to my dad about it? I'm sure he knows a lot more than I do."

"Not yet. I wanted to speak to you first. But I will, of course. This land doesn't look valuable to me, not in the first instance, but given we have no other solid leads to follow, maybe there's something we missed, something we're not seeing. We'll keep looking, regardless."

"Now I think about it, someone did approach Dad about that land. Bert Stridh. He's one of the richest people on the island."

"Okay. Thanks for the information."

Anna checked her watch. "I need to go. Is there anything else?"

"No. I'll call your dad now and ask him about this Bert Stridh."

"Great. I'll talk to him later today— maybe we can reconnect tomorrow?"

"Of course," Peter said. "Thank you for your time." He hung up.

***

Later in the afternoon, during a break from meetings, Anna video-called her father. "Dad, did the police talk to you today?"

"Hello, dear, nice to talk to you, too. How are you?"

Exasperated, Anna responded, "I'm good. Now, did the police talk to you?"

"I'm good, too. Why, thank you for asking." Anna could see how her father derived some small pleasure from this torture. "Did we not raise you to be polite?"

"Yes, Dad. Sorry. So, did Peter call you?"

"He did."

"Did he ask you about the land Pa owned?"

"Yes, and I told him. It's just worthless land out in the forest. With every new generation of Svenssons, the plots get smaller and smaller. I doubt they would be of use to anyone. There's only one place that was important to us, but not for any financial reason. It was where we used to go to when we first met, our special hideaway. Neither Lennart nor I would ever sell that plot. It's our place."

"Why didn't you mention that to me? I had no idea the land was so dear to you."

"That's not entirely true. We told you how we met many times. The fact that our secret meeting place belonged to Lennart's dad was not important to that story. He owned plots all over the island, none of them big enough to build on, and I used to wonder what the point was of paying taxes when it was worthless, but then the government abolished property taxation, and we kind of forgot about them. Now all you get is a reminder every few years that you still own it. That land in the forest is economically worthless, but it means a lot to me for sentimental reasons, maybe now more than ever."

"So what did the police have to say?"

"They wanted to know why Bert had approached me about it. As you know, I told him to forget it. The police will no doubt look into him anyway. He's always been an odd character, but I doubt he'd kill for a worthless piece of land, unless there's more to him than meets the eye." Tore shrugged. "Now, I must go. I have a doctor's appointment. Love you!"

The line disconnected before Anna could return the sentiment, and she sat back, wondering about the call. They might not be related by blood, but there was no ignoring how alike they were. *Guess the apple didn't fall that far from the tree after all.* She also couldn't shake the image of Bert from her mind. She knew him, of course. Everybody on the islands did. But she agreed with her dad. He was a creep, but a killer?

The next time she talked to the police, she learned that they didn't suspect him. It was too far-fetched. Bert had not even been on Styrsö the day of Lennart's death. He and his wife had been at their condo on the Costa del Sol. He had a daughter who worked for the city's planning department, and there had been tentative discussions about rezoning some land near Mad to allow for more construction to go ahead and make the island more viable in terms of schools, public transport, and so on.

Part of Pa's land would be involved if those plans ever went forward, but this was years into the future, and nothing was certain, given the volatility of the property market. The police found it highly unlikely, especially since the plans were public, so the finger of suspicion would naturally point to Bert. The only thing he was guilty of was trying to get ahead by buying the land in case the plans ever came to fruition. It was risky but could prove very profitable in the longer term. However, it was not illegal, and killing Lennart wouldn't have helped, as Tore would've inherited everything.

– 28 –

December 16, 2022

It was two weeks after the final pathology report before the police released Lennart's body to the family. It had been a difficult time, as the police were very tightlipped concerning the investigation. Questions were asked, often the same ones again and again, but there was little the police would tell them about potential suspects or any major leads they were following. They'd only inform them if someone was ruled out. As for active suspects? Nothing.

Organizing the funeral presented a challenge of its own. Because of the circumstances around Lennart's passing, the body was cremated on the mainland, and his ashes had been sent to the island for the funeral service. Even though a staunch atheist, Lennart had never actually left the Church and was thus eligible for a funeral service in Styrsö's beautiful white church from the 1750s. Tore and Anna had asked a family friend, a former priest in the congregation, to come to the island and lead the service. She'd readily agreed. After the funeral, they would hold a small gathering at the parish house across the street.

Tore had aged these past weeks. Having Lennart return to the island, to be reunited with him as it were, was more painful than he could've imagined. When Anna and Ali took him to the church the evening before the funeral for a private farewell, he was barely able to stay standing. His tall, beautiful man was reduced to ashes, all neatly packaged in a simple wooden urn. Tomorrow, after the service, it would be placed in the cemetery's memorial plot, along with a small plaque bearing Lennart's name and the years of his birth and death, an entire life reduced to a three-by-ten-centimeter metal plaque.

***

Sitting in the first row of the church's pews, Tore was astonished that so many people had come to take their leave of their friend and neighbor. Anna had told him they'd had to send people over to the parish house, where they could listen to the service being piped through a speaker system. Somehow, word had spread among the island's population, and curiosity had gotten the better of people who hadn't even known Lennart. Perhaps the fishermen who'd found the finger had spilled the beans, or he'd given it away at Konsum that day Anna called with the pathology report. It made no difference, not now. It wouldn't bring Lennart back. Nothing would bring him back, ever. Not as he stood there, in front of the altar amid a sea of flowers, reduced to nothing but ashes.

When Siri began the service, the atmosphere in the church was laden. Tore and Anna had asked her to keep the religious aspects light, but there were things the Church of Sweden didn't compromise on.

"Dear Tore, Anna, Ali, dear inhabitants of this peaceful and beautiful island. We gather here today with the heaviest of hearts, to take our leave of our husband, father, friend, and neighbor, Lennart Svensson. I have led many funeral services in my life, and there are always difficult ones, children, people who die of a disease or in accidents. But never have I stood with a congregation as they bury one of their own who has died so needlessly and so utterly senselessly at the hand of someone else.

"I share your anger, I share your confusion, the questions you have, one of which stands out above all others. Why? In the earthly realm, the police are searching for the answer to this very question, and we must be patient and allow them to do their work. However, as Lennart appears before our Heavenly Father, none of this matters. He will be welcomed with open arms, and he will take his place at His side. In that, we can all rejoice. Let us pray."

Siri led the congregation in prayer, after which the church choir sang "Amazing Grace," and the congregation joined in.

As a respectful silence settled once more over those gathered, Siri continued to talk about Lennart's life.

"Lennart Svensson was born on May 23, 1950, right here on the island of Styrsö in the house where he came to live most of his life. Son to Arvid Svensson and his wife, Astrid, at the age of thirteen, Lennart became an older brother when his baby sister Lena was born at Östra Sjukhuset. As a young gay man, growing up here wasn't easy, and I know he was bullied in school. Nevertheless, he persevered, worked hard to receive excellent grades, and was granted the opportunity to study in town, becoming a Chalmers engineer.

"At the time, he had already met the love of his life, Tore, who had also grown up right here on the island. In 1981, they were joined by Anna, whom Lennart had taken on as his daughter in an attempt to save his younger sister's honor."

Tore heard the whispers going through the pews as the truth of Anna's true origin was finally made public.

"It was the most selfless and heroic act by two young men, to give an innocent child a shot at happiness and a future. Anna grew up here among us and moved away to pursue her successful career as a public-relations executive in Stockholm, where she lives with her partner Ali.

"Lennart was giving in many ways. He was engaged in our local sports club, Styrsö BK, when Anna was younger and played soccer. Later in life, particularly after retirement, he would spend countless hours with his friends in the Pathfinders, restoring and maintaining the hiking trails around our beautiful island. We are many on the island who greatly appreciate the work of these selfless men and women. We thank Lennart for his service and commit his soul to the Almighty Father. Let us pray..."

The service continued with testimonies from Lennart's friends interspersed with music he'd loved. Siri had done an amazing job of capturing the raw emotion brewing on the island, the fear and the rage, and turning it into constructive mourning that everyone could partake in. After the service, Tore and Anna had to shake hands for what seemed an eternity before a smaller group finally gathered for a meal at the parish house.

Sven, who'd stayed in the background the entire time, came up to hug Anna. "I'm so sorry for your loss. I know I will miss him dearly."

"Thank you, Sven. And thanks for all the help in preparing today."

"Oh please, don't mention it. You know how much I loved Lennart. It's the least I could do."

During the meal, those who had not shared anything during the service got up and told anecdotes of their friendship with Lennart, some going back to a time even Tore didn't remember, from their school days before they'd met. Others stood up to apologize for not always having treated them well, ashamed and barely able to look Tore in the eyes as they mumbled about how those were "different times" or "we didn't know better."

Tore held no grudges; he was grateful for the love of his community, that they had found a home here, and he couldn't fathom living anywhere else. Styrsö was home, always had been, and always would be.

– 29 –

December 16, 2022

AFTER THEY HAD returned from the funeral, Tore had gone to lie down for a while. He was exhausted from all the conversations, the handshaking, and the pain of having to bury Lennart. Not knowing why someone had killed him still weighed heavily on him, the futility of the situation almost unbearable.

When they heard the front door open and Sven's voice asking if they were home, Ali went to greet him, as Anna was busy doing dishes in the kitchen. She looked up from the sink when Sven walked in behind Ali. "What are you doing here?"

"I came by to deliver the telegrams that were collected at the funeral, plus there are some leftovers. I figured you might appreciate these. Less cooking for a day or two."

"Thank you. I'm sure Dad will be grateful."

"Happy to help. How are you coping? I guess it can't be easy on you either."

"One day at a time? What can I say? Knowing your father was murdered is not easy to wrap your head around. I'm sure you can understand that."

"Yeah, totally. Have you heard anything from the police?"

"No, not in the past couple of days. Did they talk to you?"

"They did, yes. Yesterday. They wanted me to tell them the story again of that last morning, when Lennart and I were talking about renovating the shed. That's all. I think we cleared everything up."

"Did they ask you about the drawing?"

"What drawing?"

"The one you loved so much when we were kids? The one in the attic."

"Not sure I understand, but they didn't ask me about that."

"Odd, given you and Pa were the last ones up there."

Their conversation was interrupted by the ring of the doorbell—a sign that it was a stranger. Ali went to see who it was and came back with three police officers in tow, Peter Gustavson, the police inspector, leading them.

"Peter, what brings you out here this time of day?"

"Hello, Anna. We're here to arrest Sven. He's under plausible suspicion of having killed your father." Looking over at Sven, he added, "Please do not resist. We want to avoid having to use force."

Sven paled at the sight of the police officers and seemed unable to move, never mind resist. Almost robotically, he stretched out his hands and allowed himself to be cuffed.

"It was an accident! I didn't mean to." Looking at Anna, tears filled his eyes. "I'm so sorry, Anna. I don't know what got into me, but you have to believe me. It was an accident."

Anna ran upstairs to get Tore, who looked as if he'd seen a ghost when he returned with her to join the others. After everybody had taken a seat at the kitchen table, except the two police officers who stood guard behind Sven, Peter Gustavson explained why they had arrested him.

"Thanks to the assistance of Anna's manager, Anders Norén, we were able to find the flea market where they purchased the drawing. We had our local colleagues in Enköping go there today to talk to the owner, and the description the seller provided instantly led us to believe that Sven is the one who sold the drawing. They positively ID'd him when they were shown his passport photo. I would like to add this is only the beginning of the investigation. We still don't know what happened in detail or the motive for it."

Anna couldn't comprehend what she was hearing. "But you just told me you hadn't seen the drawing?"

Sven was crying, his cuffed hands folded as if in prayer, resting on the kitchen table. "Please, I can explain! It was all an accident! I didn't kill Lennart on purpose. You have to believe me!"

– 30 –

September 5, 2022

S LOWLY, AND IN great detail, Sven recounted the final hours of Lennart's life and his actions afterward.

After Tore had left to go to town and Lennart had finished in the bathroom, he had gotten busy around the house. He had done the dishes, cleaned up after them in the bathroom, and then went to work in the shed. He wanted to clear out the junk that had accumulated over the many years they had lived in the house— sell anything of value, throw away the older tools, and maybe store the rest in the attic.

Sven knew about Lennart's idea of converting the shed into a guest cabin as a surprise for Tore and a way to increase their meager pension a little bit, but Lennart had never gotten around to it. Something else had always been prioritized, but with tourism on the island growing slowly but steadily, it was the right time to do it, with the added advantage that it would stop Tore from sitting around the house now that he was retired, too. The idea of hosting guests, meeting people from other parts of the world and showing them the island where he had been born and raised, was appealing to Lennart as well. He had already begun to separate the junk from the more valuable stuff he planned to sell or intended to keep and had asked Sven to come by to help him move some of the things in the "storage" pile into the house. He didn't want to ask Tore or it would've ruined the surprise.

Sven arrived at the house at the agreed time and, as was customary, he didn't knock on the door but simply walked in. He'd done it since he was a young boy, and he wasn't the only one on the islands to do so.

Receiving no response when he called out Lennart's name, Sven closed the door again and walked around the house, heading straight to the shed. As he suspected, the door was open, the lights were on, and he heard noises from inside.

"Good morning, Lennart!" Sven smiled as he walked in. "Wow, you do mean business!"

"Morning. Yeah, I might as well get this going if we want it to be ready by summer. Thanks for helping me—and for taking the day off just for me."

"No worries. That's what friends are for. I take it this is the trash pile?"

"Yes. Some of these tools were my granddad's. They haven't been used for ages, and unless the local heritage museum wants them, we can take them to Skäret and just do away with them. Same with the timber and other junk. It contains too many nails to burn in the fireplace, and that stuff? Broken, old, useless. Where do you want to start?"

"Let's get rid of the junk first. I don't think these tools are worth saving. They're not of any special value, so I doubt the museum would want them."

They sorted the various items in the shed, what might be worth saving and what needed to be thrown out. After they were done, they moved to the house, as Lennart also wanted to check for space in the attic.

"Let's have coffee first, shall we?" he suggested. In his seventy-third year, he couldn't work too hard for too long or his body would inevitably protest. Lennart was a tall man with a thin frame, and his hair was long and snowy white. It hadn't always been white, of course, but he'd preferred to keep it long. Luckily, he'd kept a full head of hair even as it began to shift from the blond of his youth to a middle-aged mousy brown, then gray, until it had finally shifted to a bright white. Tore said he looked like a distant cousin of the dragon clan on TV. He and Tore had watched that show with great interest, never missing an episode. Sven had to chuckle at that, but Tore had a point.

"So what is it you want to do with the keepsakes?" Sven asked as Lennart poured them each a coffee into two big mugs. "And the furniture?"

"Well, I was thinking about selling the workbench. We don't need that. Some of the trinkets might eventually find their way back into the shed as decorations. As for the chairs and the table, I thought I might store those in the attic for now—if we can get them up there." Lennart tilted his head, indicating the hallway behind him. "I'm not sure it'll fit, but I don't have anywhere else to store it."

"You could ask a neighbor."

"I could, but I'd rather not. You ask for a favor, and everybody expects something in return. It's a fallback plan, though."

"I'd be happy to take the workbench off your hands. How much do you want for it?"

"You can have it. It's the least I can do for all your help." Lennart sat down and let out a heavy sigh. "That's going to hurt tonight."

"What?"

"This old body, my back." Lennart laughed. "While I'm no stranger to physical labor, I can feel that I'll be tired tonight. The lifting is getting to me."

"We can do it some other day if you like?"

"Yeah, we could do that. I'm in no hurry. At some point, I'll have to tell Tore anyway. Maybe better if I do it before we get too much work done, just in case the old coot changes his mind. But if you have the time, maybe we can start by going up to see if there's even enough space, rearrange some of what's already up there. But first, want a cookie? I'm sorry, I should've asked earlier."

"Sure. A bit of sugar wouldn't hurt."

"We don't have much. Let me see what I can find." Lennart got up again and moved over to the pantry, rummaging inside. He returned with a red roll of cookies in his hand. "S'all we have. Ballerina. They were always Anna's favorites."

"Thanks." Sven took the package from Lennart's hand. "I remember when we were kids, we would always sneak into that pantry of yours to see if there was an open pack so you guys wouldn't find out."

Lennart smiled. "Yet we always did. Then again, you two inevitably left traces, usually an empty wrapper and nothing but crumbs. And regardless of whatever new hiding places we came up with, you would find them. It was infuriating but also cute. At least, as a memory. You two made quite the couple back then."

Sven became pensive. "Yeah, but we never made that transition from friends to more. Not that I would have minded."

"I know, but it wasn't meant to be. You should move on, Sven. Anna will never see you as more than a friend."

It was the first time they'd had this kind of conversation, and Sven was surprised that Lennart knew how he felt. "You never said anything before. How come?"

"We didn't want to encourage you. You're a great guy and a great friend, but your family and ours? It wouldn't have worked. You know how bad it was with mine at the time."

Sven was puzzled. "What do you mean? What's wrong with my family?"

"You know, your religious affiliations. Your family is part of a congregation that still views us as sinners, as some erroneous entity that either needs to be eradicated or reined in, converted. Can you imagine a family dinner or celebration where those two worlds came face-to-face? I've been down that road once, with my parents, and I don't care to do it again. And I most certainly won't subject Anna to that sort of bigotry."

Sven stared at Lennart, astounded. "I have no idea what you're talking about. Why would my family have any issues with you and Tore? You've all been neighbors for decades. You guys went to school with my parents."

"Which is why I know."

"But things are different now, right?"

"If only," Lennart said wistfully.

"Has something happened since?"

"It's nothing. A run-in with your dad, that's all."

"Please," Sven insisted. "I want to know."

Lennart sighed. "I never wanted to tell you because it was painful to be treated that way, like a second-rate human, by someone whose son was best friends with our daughter. I never wanted to hurt you with that, but perhaps it would help if you understood why our two families will never be able to become one."

"Then tell me. What did he do?" Sven was becoming unnerved.

"Well, he came by to pick up an old electric pump I hadn't used in ages and was selling through our Facebook trading page. He paid me in cash and turned to leave, then suddenly, in the doorway, he stopped, turned around, looked at me, and said, 'Just because I've bought this from you doesn't mean I approve of your lifestyle. I do not. It's a sin, and things will end badly for you.' Then he turned around again and left."

"My dad said that to you?" Sven was flabbergasted.

"He sure did. That wasn't the worst I've heard in my life, but this was when you and Anna were all grown up. Tore and I had been legally married for a good decade, and it seemed as if two guys living together just wasn't a thing anymore. Alas, for some people it still is and always will be." Lennart took a deep breath, clearly upset. "Just imagine, disregarding for a moment Anna's complete disinterest in you or anything long-term, that you and she had gotten married and had kids. You'd want them baptized, right? Because your parents would expect you to do so?"

Sven nodded, though he could see Lennart was working himself up into a rage. There was a lot of pain there from the way society had treated him and Tore.

"Well, let me tell you, Sven. Anna would rather burn on a stake than have her children introduced to that sort of nonsense, to introduce them to people who despise their grandfathers. Can you picture that? And then what? How would you explain to your father and mother that your children would never be baptized?"

Sven was stupefied and struggling for words. "I, uh, but..."

"I rest my case. Let's not talk about this anymore. I'm sure you love Anna, but you need to let her go and accept she'll never be yours. Even if you could've somehow bridged the religious gap, moved away from here, and gotten out of the church's grasp, you'd still have to contend with the fact that our daughter is not interested in any relationships, not with anyone. Trust me, this has caused enough hurt and drama within these four walls over the years, and it's driven her away from us. You're a good kid, Sven. I like you. You're like a son to us. But for your own sake, forget Anna. Move on with your life. I'm sure you'll find happiness. But it won't be in this family."

Sven didn't respond, but inside him, an emotional storm was brewing, and Lennart's pity wasn't helping. This man had watched him grow up and knew how deep his feelings ran for Anna. What he hadn't realized was that Lennart, and presumably Tore, too, knew that nothing could come of it, which was something Sven had accepted long ago—on an intellectual level. *Go tell your heart!* But that was purely down to Anna's lack of interest in relationships. He hadn't known his parents had made their disapproval so obvious to Lennart.

Had Anna fallen for their neighbor's boy, there would've been immeasurable consequences, given how his church viewed same-sex relationships. Sven's mother, who was quite active in the local congregation, had often alluded to it, especially when Sven had been younger, with snide remarks about their "lifestyle" or "I'll pray for them!" No doubt his folks were as happy as Lennart and Tore that he and Anna never moved beyond the friendship level.

Inside him, something broke as the realization sank in that Lennart was right. They were never destined to become a couple. His heart finally accepted the truth, and the pain was debilitating.

"Shall we get back to it?" he asked, still in a kind of trance.

"Sure!" Lennart agreed. "Are you okay?"

Sven nodded meekly.

Lennart took the two mugs to the sink and quickly washed up, while Sven grabbed another Ballerina cookie and then followed Lennart to a narrow staircase leading up to the attic. Like the rest of the hallway, it was painted in a fading, light-gray color, and in quite a few places the paint was peeling off the wall.

Lennart climbed the stairs and stepped through the narrow door into the attic. Sven followed suit. Lennart turned on the light and then proceeded a couple more steps into the room. "Not a lot of space up here, but I think we can at least move the chairs and the table up here. We'll just have to unscrew the table's legs."

"What about the couch?" Sven asked.

"I think I'll put that on the selling list. It'll never fit up here, and I'm not sure it'll fit into the new space, either, or not the way I envision the place."

"Makes sense." Sven approached Lennart and moved to the side to get a better view of the attic. He and Anna had often played here as kids, but he hadn't been up here in decades. When he noticed the familiar frame on the dresser, he picked it up.

"I haven't seen this for ages. I always fantasized about her when I was a boy. She was the first naked woman I ever saw."

Lennart looked at the charcoal sketch of a naked young woman standing on a large boulder by the seashore. A small dinghy floated in the water next to her. It was a beautiful and very well-done sketch.

Lennart chuckled. "Nana Emilie was your jerk-off fantasy? My great-great-grandmother? You've got to be joking!" He shoved Sven with his right elbow and laughed.

Surprised by the sudden move, Sven dropped the sketch. It fell to the floor and the frame and the protective glass broke.

"Oh, I'm so sorry," he exclaimed and quickly bent down to pick it up.

"No, I'm sorry. I didn't hurt you, did I?" Lennart was genuinely concerned.

"Of course not. You caught me by surprise."

"Hang on, I'll get a broom and shovel." Watching Sven picking up the shards, he added, "Be careful. I don't want you to cut yourself."

He returned after a while with a broom only to see Sven sitting on the floor admiring the drawing, holding the paper in his hand.

"Did you know this is an Anders Zorn?"

Lennart shook his head. "You're dreaming, boy. This drawing was a present for my great-great-grandmother from her first lover. It's a long story. She had an affair when she was very young with a boy visiting the island. He was an aspiring artist, and he drew her after, you know…having had his way with her. Then he caught the ferry back into town. Nana Emilie never heard of him again, but boy did that sketch cause a lot of drama for her. She loved it and fought her parents to keep it, probably because she had a crush on the artist. Her parents found it in the drawer of her nightstand a few weeks after the fact. I'm surprised they didn't burn it. But anyway, a Zorn? No way. That's not possible. Didn't he live up in Dalecarlia and Stockholm?"

"Don't be so sure. Look at the signature. Here on the back." Sven showed it to Lennart.

"I see, but that doesn't mean it's the real deal. It could be a practical joke if you will. Mind you, I've never seen the back of the drawing before. It's always been in this frame and hanging on the wall. In fact, it used to hang on our bedroom wall, but Tore didn't much like having a naked woman look down on our private moments. We put it up here shortly after moving into the house."

Sven was still studying the signature intently. "Well, somebody signed it on the back, and the frame is quite old, so it's not impossible. You should investigate it. I once studied an art course at the university, just for fun, and I remember Zorn was in Gothenburg once, back in 1886, to start an alternative Swedish artist federation. He stayed at Hotel Eggers by the central station. When was your great-grandmother born?"

"I don't know, but it would've been around that time. Emilie was born after 1850, and the affair happened when she was just sixteen. I remember my grandmother telling me that her grandparents had unsuccessfully attempted to marry her off to someone to cover it all up, probably afraid she'd ended up pregnant. They finally found a fisherman from Fotö who took pity on her and married her. She gave birth to Elsa, my great-grandmother, their only child. My great-great-grandfather died in a storm shortly after Elsa's birth."

Sven couldn't stop looking at the sketch. "You know, if this is genuine, it could be worth a lot of money. I've never seen a charcoal sketch by Zorn. He painted, of course, and he did hundreds of etchings. You could be a long-lost descendent of Anders Zorn. How cool would that be?"

Lennart laughed dismissively. "Trust me, this is no Zorn. Someone would've found out about this in the almost one hundred and fifty years since."

"Would you mind if l looked into it?"

Lennart sighed in exasperation. "Look, we're here to work on the shed, not pursue another of your silly fantasies, and frankly, I'm growing tired of discussing a somewhat embarrassing nude drawing of one of my ancestors. I appreciate your help, boy, but you need to get your head out of the clouds. This is no Zorn, and Anna will never be yours, do you understand?"

Sven's temper flared, and he flew up from the floor to set the record straight. "Now listen," he began angrily, but as he'd gotten up so suddenly, Lennart had inadvertently taken a step back and had lost his footing. He fell backward and tumbled down the narrow flight of stairs.

It all happened in an instant. Sven didn't even have time to reach for the old man, let alone grab him. He rushed to the open door and looked down the stairs. Lennart lay, crumpled, in the narrow space at the bottom of the staircase, not moving.

"Lennart?" Sven called. "Are you okay? I didn't mean to scare you like that." He rushed down the stairs and checked if Lennart was breathing. He wasn't. He checked his pulse, but there was none to be detected. Straightening up, he stared in horror at the dead man. He'd probably broken his neck in the fall, a quick death, and it was Sven's fault, although he hadn't intended it.

He panicked. What now? Should he call the police? Emergency services? What would they say? Would he get in trouble? After all, he'd just had a fight with Lennart. His mind was reeling. He began pacing the hallway, back and forth. Every time he approached the small space where the staircase reached the hallway, he stopped, stared at the dead man lying there in a heap, then turned around again, muttering under his breath, before repeating the maneuver.

Sven paced the house for several minutes before snapping out of it. He'd killed Lennart. He hadn't intended to. It was an accident, but what did it matter to the police? Or to Tore? He'd go to jail. Anna would never forgive him. He fell to his knees and he began to wail. He was a killer.

Why did he have to come here today? Why did he have to make that stupid comment about his love for Anna? He'd had no idea this was such a contentious point for Lennart. His parents were old school, and on one level, he'd always known that Anna wouldn't fall for him. They'd discussed it years ago, after graduating from high school. Yet he couldn't help feeling the way he did. And now this!

There was a dead body lying right next to him, and he had caused it. God would never forgive him. What would Tore say when he got home? Would anyone believe him when he told them it was an accident? What if they searched the house, found the broken frame and the drawing? He was sure it was valuable, the perfect murder motive, and Anna knew how much he'd loved it. She'd say he did it for the money. He had to get rid of that, for sure, or they'd think he had done it on purpose. But what about the body? He couldn't just leave it here for Tore to find. The old man would go insane. He couldn't do that to him. He had to do away with the body somewhere. Dump it in the ocean, never to be found again. It would be easier on Tore and Anna to simply lose Lennart than to find him like this.

An idea slowly coalesced in his mind: he needed to hide the body and get rid of the sketch. Hopefully, as it had been in the attic for so long, nobody would miss it. Tore certainly wouldn't go looking for something he loathed. But what to do with Lennart's body? He needed time to think. Tore would be back in a couple of hours, and there must be no traces left. He might not find out about his visit, and if anyone had seen Sven, he could tell the truth, that he'd been here to help Lennart with the surprise. Might be the best play in the long term. Nobody would suspect him, would they? He'd known the two men all his life. This was, after all, an accident and not premeditated murder. He could never hurt a fly. He also could not let Lennart lie here like this. Tore wouldn't survive seeing him like this.

Sven cleaned up the glass and the broken frame and put them, along with the drawing, in a plastic bag. He couldn't leave them here. His fingerprints were all over it. His fingerprints would be all over the house, too, but that was easy to explain away if anyone asked. He was at the house often enough. *Stupid drawing.* Why did he have to pick it up? Yes, he did have rather fond memories of it, but those were the last thing on his mind as he focused on the difficult task at hand.

First, he needed to get the body out of there, unseen. He wrapped it into a tarpaulin from his moped and moved it to the harbor and his boat. It was just after ten in the morning, and nobody saw him. Even if they had, people transporting something on their moped under a tarpaulin was too common a sight for anyone to pay attention to it. In any case, the commuters were long gone, the kids were in school, and most of the pensioners who took the ferry to town had already left. The roads were empty. He couldn't risk waiting until dusk and Tore's return. Tore might even call him and ask him about Lennart's whereabouts.

At this stage, he was operating like a robot, programmed to execute a task. He'd completely shut off his emotions and dared not access the place in his mind where his actions were being mulled over and over. This was not the time to wrestle with his conscience.

He got lucky. There was a dense fog over the island that morning, which helped a lot, but it was already beginning to lift. Within an hour, the sun would be breaking through. Sven quickly untied his boat and steered it out of the small marina at Tången. Heading southwest, he passed Sandvik on a straight path toward Hästbåden, a couple of tiny islets along a deep canal heading out to sea. Here, he'd find water deep enough to make sure the body disappeared for good.

Arriving at a spot he saw was deep enough on the sea chart, he stopped the boat and took the anchor chain, tying it around Lennart's body. He had to make sure it stayed submerged and didn't float to the surface. He worked methodologically, detached from what he was doing. He was clearly in shock.

After having made sure that the chains sat properly around the waist and legs, he tossed the anchor overboard. With much of the chain coiled around the body, there were only a couple of meters left, and he wasn't sure if it would sink all the way to the seabed, but he'd read enough crime novels to know that decomposing bodies tended to bloat and float at some point. That mustn't happen. He slowly heaved the corpse overboard, and it disappeared into the darkness of the sea. The water was at least twenty meters deep in this spot. Nobody would come to look here. Within a couple of years, only the anchor and chain would remain, and stranger things had happened than a boat losing those.

People would likely assume Lennart had drowned after a fall. He loved to spend time at Salskärs Udde—Sven could have seen it from here, had it not been hidden by the fog—and if the old man had fallen in, his body would have been dragged out to sea by the currents, and it was a big search area. People drowned all the time, many eventually rising to the surface and washing up somewhere else entirely. With the weight of the anchor, Sven had made sure that wouldn't happen before the body had mostly decomposed. Countless crustaceans, fish, and other sea creatures would help with the task.

Returning to Tången, he tied up his boat in his regular spot and threw the frame and the glass into a neighbor's trash can but kept the drawing. He couldn't throw away something that might be a priceless work of art by one of Sweden's most famous artists, but he had to get rid of it somehow. He refused to profit from it, but the drawing needed to survive. It was a Zorn, after all.

Back home, he googled junkyards and flea markets and finally opted for one that mentioned on their website that they bought works of art. It was far enough from Gothenburg to not show up here again accidentally. He drove up there after the initial search for Lennart had been canceled and sold it for two hundred kronor. He just wanted to get rid of it. The cheap IKEA frame he'd put it in had cost him forty kronor, but it would delay or maybe completely stop anyone discovering the drawing was an Anders Zorn. The sketch was safe. It would survive to see another day.

***

"I don't understand." Those were the first words Anna uttered after Sven had finished. "If Pa fell down the stairs, why not just call the police?"

"I panicked. And I wanted to spare Tore the pain of finding him."

Tore got up and left the kitchen without saying a word. Ali followed him to make sure he'd be okay.

Anna looked at her best friend, the man she had known for decades, or thought she had, tears in her eyes. "I don't know that I'll ever be able to forgive you. I understand the accident wasn't your fault, but your actions afterward... You picked me up in the same boat you used to dump Pa in the ocean just hours earlier?" Shaking her head, she turned to the police. "Please get him out of our house!"

− 31 −

March 29, 2023

SVEN JOHANSSON WAS tried and convicted for involuntary manslaughter, crimes of peace against the grave, theft, and obstruction of justice and was sentenced to seven years in jail by Gothenburg's district court. He did not appeal the ruling.

Tore and Anna did not attend the proceedings.

The charcoal drawing of Nana Emilie was donated to the Zorn Museum in Mora, where it was first to be displayed to a wider public in a special exhibit sponsored by Anna's employer. The plaque under the drawing's frame named Anna and Tore as the donors.

– EPILOGUE –
Midsummer 2023

I'M SO GLAD you decided to celebrate Midsummer here with me!" Tore hugged Anna warmly, having come down to Styrsö Tången to welcome her home.

"So are we. I think we'll be lucky with the weather, too. The forecast has nothing but sunshine in store for the entire weekend." Anna was positively glowing as her father released her to greet her partner.

"Hello, Ali, so good to see you again, son. How was your trip?"

"It was good, thanks, Tore."

"Dad, I insist. You must call me Dad. We're family, after all." The older man put his arm around Ali's shoulder and beamed with pride.

Together, they walked back to the house, Ali carrying the bags for their stay while Anna and Tore took the lead, chatting with each other. A lot of people had gotten off the boat with them, but within minutes, silence descended upon the island again, and all one could hear were the noises of boat engines roaring through Snobbrännan, the cries of seagulls sailing through the sky above, and happy voices and music coming from some of the gardens.

"How long are you staying?" Tore asked.

"At least a week. We're on vacation, and we don't have any other plans. We're playing it by ear."

"That's great. I've been looking forward to having you close again. It's been so empty in the house, you know, since..." Tore didn't have to finish for Anna to know what he meant. "But I do have a surprise for you."

"What? Tell me!"

Tore laughed. "No, or it won't be a surprise."

"Okay, you win—for now. Have you spoken to the lawyer about Pa's estate yet?

"I have, but let's not ruin Midsummer with that now, okay? I'm just glad to have my girl and her partner home for now. We'll have plenty of time to talk about that next week."

"Sounds like a plan."

They walked the remaining distance home, and as they approached the gate, Tore stopped Anna and Ali. "Wait here! I need to go fetch something." He disappeared into the house, leaving Anna and Ali to exchange meaningful glances. From inside, they could hear barking. Anna smiled.

"Dad got himself a dog?"

***

The next morning, Midsummer's Eve, Anna woke up early. She felt weird and queasy and barely made it to the bathroom. Ali didn't stir. Deciding to let him sleep, she got dressed and went back to brush her teeth before going downstairs for a cup of coffee. She knew her father would already be up. He was sitting at the kitchen table with the dog, a cute black Labradoodle called Ludde, by his side, wagging his tail as he saw the latest member of his pack walk into the kitchen.

"Good morning, sunshine! How are you today?" Tore asked, petting the dog so he wouldn't bark at her.

"Not good! I just threw up. Do you think it might have been the shrimp we ate last night?"

"Nah, I can't imagine that. You know I always get them fresh right off the boat. Do you want some tea?"

"I'd rather have a cup of coffee."

"You sure? On an upset stomach? I think a cup of chamomile tea might be better."

Anna gave in. He did have a point. "Okay, chamomile tea it is."

Tore put on the water heater and got the tea bags from the pantry, Ludde following his every step. "Are you sure you're okay and it's not another one of those Covid strains? I got another booster recently, but I still don't want to catch that bug again."

"How am I supposed to know that? I haven't had a cold or cough, and I have no fever." She shrugged. "Not to mention that my sense of smell seems intact."

"How are things between you and Ali?" Tore brought a tea mug from one of the cupboards and set it on the table in front of her.

"Great. I never thought I'd say this, but this relationship is the best thing that ever happened to me." She grinned, and Tore put his hand on her shoulder.

"I am so very happy for you. The two of you certainly look happy. How are things going with his medical license?"

"It's moving at a glacial pace. It's so annoying, but I get it. Nobody wants to find out their doctor is a quack. Haafiza managed to provide us with some of his university transcripts, so now we have actual evidence that he went to medical school in Syria, but it's still a long way to go. He's currently enrolled in a special class—Swedish for medical staff. Who knew that was a thing?" She rolled her eyes. "I mean, he speaks better Swedish than many locals I know. But it's a requirement, so again, no choice but to go with the flow."

"Maybe it's not such a bad thing. It allows you to get to know each other better. Once he's working for a hospital or whatnot, you'll barely see him, what with the crazy hours they have to work. What about you? How's the hunt for another job going?"

"I've been in talks with a couple of agencies around the country. It's a slow process. I'm in no hurry. But there is one place that I would like to get into."

Tore looked up at her. "Country? You're not just looking in Stockholm?"

That had Anna smiling. Before the trip, she hadn't been sure she was ready to tell him they were contemplating a move back to Gothenburg. Now she was.

"Nope, I don't think Stockholm is my city. It's just never become home, you know?"

"Home?" Tore repeated.

"Yeah, home." She looked around the room and back at her dad. "Home."

The water was done heating, and Tore poured it into the mug, then added the tea bag. Within seconds, the delicate smell of the chamomile reached her nostrils, and she ran off to the guest toilet on the ground floor.

When she came back, Tore was sitting at the kitchen table again, one hand cuddling Ludde's head, as he looked up at his beautiful daughter, grinning broadly, and asked casually, "Tell me, dear, when was your last period?"

The End

– ACKNOWLEDGEMENTS –

Another book is done. My first thanks need to go to a writer friend of mine, Eva Rehbinder, who inspired me to look closer to home in terms of writing after I had read her biography, *Rapport från ett liv på övertid*. Not only did I greatly enjoy reading about her life, beautifully written, but I also got engrossed in her descriptions of life here on Styrsö in the early 1980s.

The second thank-you is to my foreign readers. Not once have I met a reader who, after answering the question of where I was from, didn't ask if I wrote crime. Well, in my twenty-seventh work, I finally gave in and did it. I hope you liked it. Another Swedish writer wrote a crime novel. I hope you're pleased...

Given all the local research that has gone into this book, I owe a debt of gratitude not only to the many people on the island that I have spoken to about this or that, too many to mention by name. While each of their contributions may be tiny, put together, it made the story possible. However, there are a few names that must be mentioned: the heritage foundation of Styrsö (Styrsö Hembygdsförening); our beloved Pathfinders, or Stigfinnarna as they're called in Swedish; Carina Gustafsson and Johanna Hellström at the Missing Persons Unit at the Gothenburg Police, who provided me with the necessary information about police work. I hope I haven't screwed things up. A special thanks to Markus Jielin, my former personal trainer, who works as a police officer today, and who provided me with additional information.

As has become custom, I owe a great debt of gratitude to my publisher, Beaten Track Publishing, for indulging me on yet another journey into a new world, for a stunning cover and all the work that goes into editing, proofing, typesetting, formatting, paging, and preparing a book for sale around the world.

To say that I am indebted to my editor Debbie McGowan is the understatement of this century. Her love for writing and her care for every manuscript she reads and works on allows me to relax as I await her valuable feedback, knowing I'm in the best hands possible. To be able to call her a friend is a bonus I cherish greatly. Ten years and counting...

I'm also indebted to my alpha readers Kim, Tracy, and Alex, who read a very early and rough version of the manuscript to make sure that it worked. To write a crime novel, as much as it is done my way, was a scary endeavor, and writing a female lead even more so. I'm glad they felt I should continue. A big thank-you to proofreaders and everyone else involved in turning a simple word-processing file into a beautiful book. I'm always amazed at the outcome.

Finally, a great thanks to my family for continuing to indulge me in my writing, giving me the headspace and the peace of mind to do my research and focus on my characters and the stories they tell me. I love you!

− ABOUT THE AUTHOR −

Hans M Hirschi writes hopeful character-driven stories where ordinary people have to deal with unexpected situations making the spectrum of queer lives visible to a wider public. There's a reason why he's been dubbed The Queen of Unconventional Happy Endings.

Photo: Alina Oswald, New York

He lives in the Gothenburg archipelago with his husband, son, and pets. When not writing, he works as a learning and development executive and VIP tour guide.

Visit Hans online at: www.hirschi.se

— BY THE AUTHOR —

Adult Fiction

Novels

Family Ties

The Opera House

Living the Rainbow – A Gay Family Triptych
(includes *Family Ties*, *The Opera House*, and *Jonathan's Hope*)

The Fallen Angels of Karnataka

Willem of the Tafel

Ross Deere – Handy Man

Last Winter's Snow

Disease

Matt: More Than Words

Michel – Fallen Angel of Paris

Anna and the Lost Zorn

The Jonathan Trilogy

Jonathan's Hope

Jonathan's Promise

Jonathan's Legacy

Short Stories

Shorts – Stories from Beneath the Rainbow

Clara
(part of the *Never Too Late* anthology)

A Christmas Miracle
(*The Opera House* short story)

Young Adult Fiction

Spanish Bay

The Golden One
Blooming
Deceit
Reckoning

Children's Fiction

Valerius and Evander
The Dragon Princess
Felix and the Orphanage
The Vampire Who Lost Her Fangs

Non-Fiction

Dads – A Gay Couple's Surrogacy Journey in India
Common Sense – In Business & Life

− BEATEN TRACK PUBLISHING −

For more titles from Beaten Track Publishing,
please visit our website:

https://www.beatentrackpublishing.com

Thanks for reading!